REDEEMING
TIME

REDEEMING TIME

THE KAIROS FILES | BOOK THREE

K.S. HALL

ISBN: 978-0-9995308-9-4

This book is dedicated to Stephen Cromar Hintze.

Thank you for being the best brother a girl could ever have.
Fly with the angels... until we meet again.

ONE

GRACE

"It's a gift from my new friend." Mom's cheeks turn slightly pink as she grins at me like a school girl. "I was going to tell you about him as soon as you returned from your little trip with Jillian."

I plop down on the sofa in the living room of my brownstone. I hadn't been here in months and I take a deep breath, my head spinning. I glance around at the room. The familiar sofa and rug underneath my feet grounds me to my new reality. I'm home. I'm safe. Now I get to make sure my mom is safe, also. I clasp the ruby necklace tightly in my palm as her words sink in.

Swallowing, I try to remain calm. Xavier Castillo is her *friend?* What the heck! He's the leader of the Vagaries and a dangerous enemy of the Kairos. Mom has only been on a few dates since my dad died. How dare Xavier Castillo use her like this? I guess I shouldn't be surprised at the lengths to which the Vagaries will stoop.

"May I ask his name?" Dante asks politely. He squeezes my hand as he's sees I'm about to explode. Dante, the handsome guy who introduced me to the Kairos, remains outwardly calm, but his eyes narrow slightly and a muscle tightens along his jaw.

"Well, he's kind of an important man," Mom says. "I met him in the ER after he'd been mugged. I tell you, what is this city coming to that a person can't even walk down the street anymore without fear of being attacked? Anyway, he came to the hospital and I treated his black eye and a cut on his cheek. He was so grateful that he brought me a coffee after work. His name is Xavier Castillo and he's very nice."

I jump from my chair and turn to Dante. He stands also. His blue eyes are filled with anger and a determination I've come to recognize. We *have* to tell Mom about Xavier Castillo, the Kairos, the group of time-travelers I've become involved with, everything. There is so much she doesn't know. It's too dangerous, especially now that Xavier has made contact with her.

The front door flies opens and Henry rushes into the room, tossing his back pack on the chair by the door. He stops short when he sees me and Dante.

"Henry!" I rush over and pull him into a tight hug. It feels *so* good to hug my little brother. I wasn't sure if I'd ever see him again. He submits to my embrace for a moment then wiggles free.

"I'm hungry. Do we have any cookies?"

"I have some in the kitchen," Mom says, ruffling his hair. She turns to Dante and smiles. "I'll be right back." We watch them leave the room.

"We *have* to tell her," I whisper intensely. "I won't let Xavier hurt my family."

"You're right, of course." Dante rakes his hands through his dark hair. "Vivica won't like it, but I think the best solution is to take them to Kairos house. They'll be safe there."

I nod, my hands twisting together. Vivica, the leader of the Kairos in New York City, is very protective of the time-travelers and guards their secrecy at all costs. I wonder how much my best friend Jillian knows about where I've been the last few months? I'm dying to talk to her, although I'm sure Jacob will have filled her in somewhat.

Mom's laughter rings out from the kitchen and a wash of love flows over me. I have a lot to discuss with my mom. Namely Clara. Is she really my biological mother? What will she think when she finds out Clara's been alive all this time, stuck fifty years in the future? It's all such a tangled web. I need answers.

Mom returns to the living room. She's all smiles, her eyes bright.

"We need to talk," I say, and gesture for her to sit down. She raises an eyebrow but sinks onto the sofa. I can tell by the look on her face she thinks that I object to her dating again. She's in for a big surprise.

"I'd like to tell you how I met Dante," I says, taking his hand in mine. "If you'll wait until I'm finished, I'll answer any of your questions."

Mom nods, eyes widening.

"I met him in quite an unusual way. I know this is going to sound weird, but I promise this is true." I take a deep breath and glance at Dante before continuing. "I had accidentally time-traveled to a warehouse fire in 1913. Dante was there on an assignment to save as many people as possible. He was shocked to see a girl from our time there, also. He brought me back to the present with him. I'm a time-traveler, Mom, as is Dante."

Mom shakes her head, eyes wide. "What are you talking about? Is this some kind of a joke?"

"It's true, Mom. Dante saved my life. He's part of a secret organization of time-travelers called the Kairos. They work to keep our world safe. That's why I've been so...preoccupied lately. I'm a Kairos now, too."

"Unfortunately, there are other travelers who are not so noble," Dante adds. "They work for their own power and interests. They call themselves, Vagaries, and their leader is a man named Xavier Castillo. He's a ruthless and power hungry man and he's after Grace."

4

"He's using you, to get to me. We have to protect you and Henry."

"I need you to come to Kairos house for a while. You'll be safe there while we take care of this threat," Dante says, grimly.

I hold up the necklace. "This is proof, Mom. This necklace is a threat. I was wearing this yesterday at a masquerade ball given by Castillo, in the year 2068."

Mom eyes the necklace then rubs her forehead. "This is all so hard to believe. Time-travel? Villains after you.. really Grace."

"I know it's a lot of information to process. Please come with us, Mrs. Bennet. I can explain more when we get there," Dante says. His bright blue eyes are serious as he gazes intently at my mom.

"So, he was using me to get to you, Grace?" Mom asks, pain in her eyes. I nod slowly. I hate to see her hurt.

"I guess I have no choice but to believe you." She wipes a shaking hand down her face.

"I feel like such a fool. I knew it was too good to be true," Mom says, shaking her head. She takes a deep breath. "I suppose I had better go with you then. I must admit this seems like the stuff of science fiction or something." Mom glances at me once more as if willing me to tell her it was all a crazy joke. I just nod.

"I'll get Henry ready then," she says, rising to her feet.

5

"It would be best if you pack an overnight bag," Dante says, rubbing the back of his neck, a sure sign of the tension he's feeling. "You too, Grace. I don't want you coming back here until we know what Castillo is up to. You are all in danger unprotected here."

Mom's mouth drops open. "Danger? Isn't that a bit extreme?" She shakes her head in disbelief. I nod and squeeze her hand.

"I guess I'll go get Henry ready then. We had better go with you," she says. I think she has finally realized that we are serious about this.

I sigh, relieved. I know this is hard to for her to believe. It took me a long time to accept the reality of time travel, also. Years really, when you consider all the incidences that I'd had as a child. Time-travel is just *one* of the shocks she'll receive today, I think, remembering Clara.

Dante pulls his cellphone from his coat pocket and calls Bruce. He instructs him to bring the car to my house. I glance into the kitchen where Mom is stashing the package of cookies into the cupboard. Henry glances in my direction as she explains that we are going out. His shoulders slump.

"But I wanted to play video games," he whines. Poor kid. Life for my family will never be the same once they become entangled with the Kairos.

I had better go pack a few things also, I think, and I pick up my backpack. The weight of the bag reminds me that it's far from empty. Along with my few personal items, it contains the Ambitus, the Flag of MacLeod, and the Golden Chalice. Liam promised to guard Excalibur for me. I couldn't let this backpack out of my sight, though. We were lucky to have found these ancient treasures that allowed us to return to the present day.

"I'll be right back," I say. Dante nods. His eyes softening, and he smiles as he looks at me. I return his smile. It's so good to be home.

I cross the hall and enter my bedroom. Everything looks the same. Somehow I thought it would be different. I've been gone for months, but in this reality it's only been a few days. I pull the overnight bag from the top shelf of my closet and stuff some clothes inside along with my undies and a small toiletry bag.

I suddenly have a thought that has me sinking onto the bed. What about high school? I'm supposed to graduate in a few months. Will I be allowed to finish my senior year? One more thing I'll have to figure out, I guess. I've been through so much in the last two months. I learned I could travel through time, met Dante, my new time-traveling boyfriend, and was stalked by Marco. He ended up dead, thanks to the Ambitus, and now Xavier Castillo is after me and the abilities I have to control this powerful dagger.

I shake my head and gaze slowly around the room. I look for anything else I might need. I notice the little Egyptian beetle sitting on the corner of my desk. I cross the room and slowly pick it up, its head bobbing. Marco gave this to Henry in an attempt to frighten me. It worked. Holding it in my hand, the little trinket still holds the same power of intimidation. My family isn't safe from the Vagaries. I know this more than ever now. I touch the smooth surface of the bone before carefully placing the ancient toy back onto the desk. I pick up my bags. It's time to face whatever the future holds.

CHRISTIAN

I stand in the vast hallway of Kairos house and examine my surroundings. This place is too formal and makes me nervous. I shift uncomfortably from one foot to the other, feeling out of place. A huge crystal chandelier hangs in the massive two story entrance. Black and white marble is inlaid with an intricate mosaic of the Kairos symbol. The letter K is prominent in the center. An eagle in flight, clutching the world in its talons flies above it, while an Uroboros, a serpent swallowing its own tail, circles the entire mosaic. This whole place is over the top. It's certainly different than the underground caves our small band of Kairos hid in Missouri... fifty years in the future. I grimace at the memories.

The distant sounds of the city filter through the windows,

interrupting my dark thoughts. Horns blare and brakes squeal. Leon would have loved to see this place. My shoulders drop as I think of my childhood friend. He came so close to making it here. Unfortunately, even the healing powers of the portal couldn't save him. The clean-up team took care of him. His body was moved to a cemetery on a small island in the south pacific where all the Kairos are buried. At least he has a peaceful resting place.

I peer through a window. The statue of Atlas holding up the world looks imposing in the middle of the courtyard. The iron gate is open wide and I notice the Kairos leaders, Vivica and Quinton, standing at the entrance. We were introduced to them as soon as we traveled to this house. They were polite, but I wouldn't exactly say welcoming. Vivica is coolly beautiful, but stony at the same time. That is one uptight chick. She probably has good reason for her cold manner as the Vagaries and the Kairos are on the brink of war.

A large black car pulls up to the curb. The door opens and Dante O'Rourke climbs out of the front seat. He opens the back door and Grace steps onto the curb beside him. She's looks gorgeous in the afternoon light, and I move back from the window out of sight. My heartbeat speeds up. I haven't seen her since we travelled to Kairos house. She chose to immediately go to her family before coming here.

The driver helps a pretty middle-aged woman with dark hair from the car followed by a little boy. He must be Grace's brother, Henry. The driver opens the trunk and retrieves several bags.

I step aside as Juanita, the housekeeper, brushes past me and flings open the door. The group is moving towards us and I suddenly wish I was anywhere but here.

"Wow, this place is awesome," Henry says as he rushes through the door.

I lean casually against the wall and try to look at ease, but I'm anything but relaxed. I remind myself of everything that's happened in the past months. I'm Christian Pierce. I know who I am and where I've come from. I'm a member of the Kairos and I deserve to be here.

Once everyone is inside, Juanita shuts the door and announces, "I've just put on a fresh pot of coffee. I'll bring it to the great room, if you'd like to make yourselves comfortable."

At Vivica's nod, Juanita exits the room.

Grace steps forward and slips her arm through the arm of the dark haired woman by her side. They look a lot alike.

"Vivica, Quinton, I'd like you to meet my mother, Linda Bennet, and my little brother, Henry." Vivica nods her head while Quinton steps forward and shakes Linda's hand.

"We're glad you're here. We have much to discuss. May I suggest we move to the comfort of the great room?" He gestures down the hall toward the back of the house. I wonder if they even know I'm here. I'm about to make a quick exit when Grace crosses the room towards me.

"Christian, how are you? Did someone show you around?"

I shrug, effecting an unconcerned air. "Yeah, Matthew gave everyone a tour as soon as we arrived. A lot of us are hanging out in the training room downstairs. That's a nice setup they've got there."

I gaze into Grace's bright amber eyes. *Play it cool, she's got a boyfriend.* I remind myself. Just because you became close friends during your escape doesn't mean you have any claim now.

"That's good," Grace says. "These kindred are the best. I'm sure you'll fit right in." She smiles, her hand touching my arm. I look down and notice the wound on my arm is almost gone. I had cut myself for the blood needed to open the portal.

"It looks better," Grace says, gently touching the red line.

"It's fine," I shrug, dropping my arm.

"Okay. I'll see you later," she whispers before following the group down the hall and out of sight.

I release a breath and glance out of the window once more. The driver is closing the gate and securing the lock. The danger is real here, too. We might be safe at the moment, but I know that things can change in a heartbeat. I'll keep my guard up. I'm not taking any chances, especially in a city I'm not familiar with. I'm might be a trained fighter, but the rules of the battle keep changing and I need to adapt with them.

Avery, one of my Kindred from Missouri, appears in the door that leads to the basement. She's smoothed her long blonde hair into a ponytail and is dressed in workout gear.

"There you are," she says, slightly out of breath. She wipes a film of sweat from her forehead and smiles brightly. "Liam and Jacob are teaching us how to use some of the ancient weapons. Come on. You don't want to miss it."

I shrug and glance around. It might feel good to work off some excess energy.

"Lead the way," I say, and hold out my hand. She takes it with a giggle and pulls me down to the basement.

The clang of sword play grows louder as we near the bottom of the stairs. Avery flings open the door and we step inside. A large black man, who was introduced as Liam, wields a sword with ease. A strikingly beautiful red-haired girl leaps out of the way as his sword swishes past her head. I'd noticed her earlier but was never introduced. She spins and meets the parry of her opponent head on. The blades sing as they hit metal on metal.

"Nice move, Scarlet," Liam says, raising his weapon once more.

"Hey, you're not taking it easy on her, are you?" asks Jacob, another Kairos who lives in the house.

Scarlet points her sword at Liam. "You'd better not!" she scolds with a teasing smile. I notice these are tipped epee's used for practice and feel slightly better. One wrong move and there could have been a serious injury.

I've never been much for swords. Kickboxing and hand to hand fighting, and a knife tucked discreetly in my boot, perfected on the streets of Kansas City, is more my style.

Raymond sits at the end of the room, hands on knees, watching the sparring. Trina and Alejandro lean against the opposite wall. Alejandro, who has always had a thing for knives, is practically drooling.

"Crazy, right?" Avery whispers, her eyes sparkling with excitement. "We need to learn how to use all this stuff now that we're going on assignments with the Kairos."

Going on assignments? I hadn't thought that far ahead. At the moment, I just want to make it through today.

There are all kinds of weapons lining the far wall. Cross bows and nunchucks along with several wicked looking quarterstaff poles. Axes and knives lay on a nearby shelf ready for any kind of battle. My reaction is less enthusiastic. I'll wait and reserve judgement. The weapons are impressive, but I've been used as a weapon to fight before, and I'm not too excited to repeat the experience.

Matthew enters the gym. "Juanita sent me down to tell you she has refreshments in the kitchen when your finished down here."

Avery immediately moves to stand beside him. Matthew was the one who gave us the tour of the house when we first arrived. He seems like a straight forward, no nonsense kind of guy.

I flex my shoulders and roll my neck. I haven't worked out in a few days and I'm itching to punch something. Maybe

Matthew would be up for it.

"Do you ever practice hand to hand combat?" I ask him.

"Sure, I'm game," he says.

I nod. Matthew has the advantage as he's bigger than me by at least fifty pounds and four inches taller, but I'm strong and quick. Hopefully my street moves will even the odds.

We meet in the center of the room as everyone clears a space for us. I flex my arms and stretch as I begin to walk lightly around Matthew. He stands still his eyes following my every move. He seems calm and relaxed, like a cobra ready to strike at any moment. Maybe I was a bit premature to take on this hulk of a guy. His fist suddenly shoots out and I dance to the side, his strike barely missing my face.

I swing my leg out in a round house move to kick his knee, but he jumps to the side and whirls to face me. He lifts his chin, nodding, like he's surprised to find I'm a worthy opponent.

I follow this with a karate kick, making contact with his mid sections. He barely moves and he doesn't seem fazed. Okay then. He's a really strong guy. His eyes narrow and I figure he's deciding where to strike next. I swallow. I won't allow any fear to get to me. My hands close into fists. I'm ready for him.

We dance around each other, well matched. Lightning fast, Matthew's arm swings away. I jump forward kicking my leg out and catching him in the back of the knee. His leg buckles and he falls. I join him on the mat, attempting a wrestling head lock. He bucks a few times. With his larger body mass, he manages to throw me off without too much effort. He scrambles to his feet and I quickly follow. We stare at each other, waiting for the next move.

Quinton Langley steps in the room and raises a hand.

"Enough sparring for today. Vivica wants you cleaned up and ready for the house meeting." He glances from me to Matthew, and grins. "It's nice to see Christian give you a run for your money, Matthew."

Matthew shrugs, but steps forward hand outstretched. I shake his hand firmly and he says, "I'll fight alongside you any day."

"Same here, man," I agree, nodding. He's a great fighter and seems like a nice guy. I realize I have a lot of adjusting to do, learning to trust these new Kairos.

Scarlet stands next to her brother and nods at me approvingly.

"Since you guys came here with nothing but the clothes on your back, let's go to the wardrobe closet and see what we can find that fits you," she says. Avery looks positively ecstatic at the prospect.

We follow her up the stairs. I hate accepting other people's handouts, but I swallow down my pride and admit it will be nice to meet the rest of the Kairos in something other than my grimy workout clothes.

THREE

GRACE

Vivica and Quinton lead us to the great room at the back of the house. I sit on the edge of the large sofa next to Mom and Henry. Vivica and Quinton take a seat in the chairs opposite. I grip the soft linen of the sofa and take a deep breath. The smell of lemon furniture polish mixes with the fresh roses on the table between us.

"I assume Grace has told you about the Kairos," Vivica says.

"She's told me some things, yes," Mom replies, her eyes huge in her pale face. A pang of guilt clogs my throat. Mom's whole world is about to turn upside down. Time-travel is a lot to digest. It took me months to accept who I was. Not to mention the fact that there's a battle for world domination happening right now and we're right in the middle of it.

Juanita enters with a tray of coffee and blueberry scones, setting it on the coffee table in front of the sofa. My stomach rumbles appreciatively. Food was a long time ago. Henry snatches up the flaky pastry, stuffing half of it into his mouth in one bite. Several crumbs land on the expensive carpet. I grimace.

"Perhaps Henry would enjoy some hot chocolate in the kitchen," Vivica says, motioning toward the door.

"Of course," Juanita replies, "I have some cookies just out of the oven, too."

Henry looks questioningly at Mom, and at her nod of encouragement, he follows Juanita from the room. Quinton clears his throat and leans forward, brow creased.

"The Kairos are very private. We normally don't share our existence with…others. This is a difficult time for us. Your safety and the future of all humanity is at stake and so we felt it necessary to bring you here."

"Grace has an extraordinary gift. One that is quite valuable to our kind. So much so that it has brought the attention of the Vagaries upon her, and thus on you," Vivica adds, gesturing to mom. "We've called a meeting of the Kairos tonight. I suggest you relax in Scarlets room tonight. This meeting is for Kairos only. We will discussing important information best restricted to our kind."

I want to object and protest that Mom needs to know everything, too, but perhaps Vivica is right. Maybe it's best to keep Mom ignorant of our plans as to not risk the details falling into the Vagaries hands. Just the idea of the Vagaries getting to my mom makes my stomach clench in protest.

"So all this is true?" Mom asks, "You really can travel through time?"

Vivica nods. Mom glances at me like I've suddenly grown another head.

"I know it's a shock. We keep ourselves hidden for that very reason," Vivica says

"I've travelled a few times as a kid, I just didn't know what was happening," I say. Mom's eyes widen. "I remember some of your crazy stories but I just thought you had a vivid imagination," she says, shaking her head. "I had no idea."

"Grace has the ability to control some powerful ancient treasures. One of the pieces is priceless to our kind," Vivica says. "It carried her fifty years into the future."

She slowly stands and walks to a set of sliding doors on the other end of the room. "She met someone there who has been waiting anxiously to see you."

Vivica slides the door open and Clara steps into the room. She's beautiful in a slim green

dress, a wide brown leather belt at her waist. Her dark brown hair flows in soft curls over her shoulder. Mom slowly rises to her feet, a trembling hand covering her mouth.

"Linda. My dear, sister," Clara cries, holding out both hands. They fly across the space between them and embrace in a fierce hug. When they finally part, they're both crying.

"I thought you were dead," Mom says, wiping her cheeks with both hands.

"I was trapped in the future. There was no way to get word to anyone where I was or what had happened."

They sit beside each other on the sofa, Mom's hand clasped tight in Clara's, their dark heads close together. I swallow hard, at the lump in my chest. If the things Castillo told me in Missouri are true, Clara is my biological mother.

"I'm happy to see you sisters reunited, but now we have a delicate subject we must discuss." Vivica says. "Travelling can be hereditary and runs in families." She glances questioningly at Clara and then at Mom. I stand to face them.

"I love you both very much, but I need answers." I swallow and rub my sweaty palms on my pants. "One of you is my Mother and one of you is my Aunt. I deserve to know the truth."

Clara and Mom look at each other. Mom nods, and squeezes Clara's hand before whispering, "Go ahead."

Clara hesitates, gathering her thoughts. "I wanted to tell you so many times in the past few months, but I didn't want to hurt you," she says. She stands, and walks to the window before turning to face the room.

"You were born in Paris in 1888. We'd been in a battle over several pieces of prime real estate in Manhattan. My assignment was to get close to Simon Hayes and discover the

Vagaries next move. Neither of us expected to fall in love. I was a Kairos spy. Your father was the leader of the Vagaries. We were supposed to be enemies." She sighs and gazes out of the window as if reliving that time.

"But love wants what it wants. Imagine my shock when I learned I was pregnant. How could I protect you? You were a vulnerable baby. The only thing I could think to do was hide you. But who could I trust with my child? Fortunately, I had kept my family life separate from my life with the Kairos. I prayed it would be enough."

I swallow hard and clasp my hands tightly together. It's true then. Clara is my biological mother.

"When you were a month old I went to Linda and Daniel and asked them to raise you. I never told them the truth… only that I wasn't ready for the responsibility of a child. Linda disapproved, of course. I let her believe it was because I was a free spirit, a gypsy who didn't want a baby to cramp her style. It broke my heart to have her think of me that way, but your safety depended on it. I knew they had been struggling with infertility and so they agreed to raise you as their own. I purchased the brownstone and deposited all of the money I could gather into an account for you and Linda. I wanted to make sure you would have everything you needed."

Mom slips her hand in mine, her eyes round. This is new information to her also.

"You're the best thing that ever happened to me, Grace,"

Mom says. "I didn't know until now the real reason Clara gave you to me, but I'm grateful that she did. You will always be my daughter, sweetheart." Her voice hitches on a sob, and she pulls me close. Fat tears fall down my cheeks as I return the embrace.

After a few moments Clara speaks, her voice strained as she continues her story. "I left you with Linda and fled to Kairos house, heartbroken. How could I go on? Simon had gone into hiding, I had no idea where. I was on the run and the Vagaries were searching for us. I had just left my baby with my sister and I didn't know when I'd see her again. I was devastated and terrified. When I arrived at Kairos house, I found Vivica working with her Ambitus. I poured out as much of my heartbreak to her as I dared, only saying that I'd fallen in love and that it was over." Vivica nods as Clara glances her way and continues.

"The next thing I knew I was hurtling through time, into an unknown future. I was taken away from the heartbreak, yes, but found myself in more pain than I could ever have imagined. I've learned a valuable lesson during the last eighteen years. Never run from your problems. Face them head on." Clara glances around the room at Vivica, Quinton and Linda, her gaze finally settling on me.

I glance from Mom to Clara, two amazing women, both my mothers. I realize they both love me and only want the best for me. I stretch out my arms to include them both. They rush forward and hug me tightly, a Grace sandwich. The ticking clock on the fireplace mantle is the only sound, besides a few sniffles from our embrace.

"We should get ready for the house meeting now. We can talk more later," Vivica whispers after a moment.

Clara lets go first, wiping her face on her sleeve, and I gaze into her eyes, so much like my own. I suddenly remember the Swiss bank account numbers but now isn't the time to get into that. There will be more to discuss later.

"I need to know if Simon is still alive somewhere," Clara says, her voice full of determination. She squares her shoulders and adds, "I intend to stop Xavier Castillo… once and for all."

FOUR

CHRISTIAN

I pull at the neck of the blue button down shirt Jacob lent me. It's a little tight and the sleeves are too short, but I'm not complaining. At least the clothes are clean and I just ate the best meal I've had in a long while. Food was pretty scarce in Missouri. Hell, even the basic necessities were hard to find with the Vagaries running things. It's how they controlled the people.

Trina and Avery walk behind me. They admire Kairos house, eyes wide as they glance around. Trina is dressed in a red silk blouse and black skirt and she suddenly looks older than her fifteen years.

"You clean up well," Avery whispers, leaning close as we head down the stairs for the house meeting. She's dressed in

24

black skinny jeans and a silver sweater, the fit accentuating her curves. Her blonde hair is pulled into a high ponytail and diamond earrings dangle from her ears. She's gorgeous and she knows it.

I whistle softly and say, "You'll be breaking hearts in no time."

She smiles, slipping her arm through mine as we cross the hall to the great room where the meeting is to be held. The room is filled with people already and the low hum of conversations as the Kairos gather in small groups. I shrug away the nerves and square my shoulders. These people are supposed to be my Kindred, but I'll wait and see how this all plays out. I don't trust easily these days.

"Ay, Dios mio," Alejandro whispers in my ear and I whirl to face him.

"Don't sneak up on me like that. You almost had my fist in your face."

He grins, and shrugs. "Did you see all the pretty girls, man? I think I'm going to like it here."

I turn and survey the room. There *are* some pretty girls here, but it's not surprising as the Kairos are known for their good looks.

Alejandro's gaze settles on a striking olive-skinned girl. She's dressed in dark jeans and a V-neck long sleeve shirt, with long black hair and dark eyes. She's also Hispanic, like Alejandro, and a total knockout. I wonder if she's from New York City or traveled here from a another country.

"I have to meet her," Alejandro whispers.

I shrug, nodding. I've no interest in the complications girls would bring at the moment. Now that I'm certain Grace and I are not happening, I'll focus on defeating the Vagaries.

The room is full of Kairos, some that I've just met that live in the house and many more from other cities and counties. I notice a few people in Sari's and Dhoti, the traditional dress of India. There are groups from Asia, Africa and Eastern Europe.

A door at the side of the room opens and Vivica, Quinton and Clara emerge, followed by Grace and Dante. Grace looks lovely in a dark blue dress and white sweater and I look away quickly. I don't want to be caught staring. The murmur of voices dies down as Vivica moves to address the crowd.

"Thank you for coming at such short notice, Kindred. As you may have heard, the portals to the future have been opened at last. While this is certainly good news, it also complicates our ongoing conflict with the Vagaries. At this moment we have no further information on what their next move will be. We will be scouting the city for clues as to their next move. We have no doubt they will be planning something."

A few people whisper, but quiet down as Vivica continues.

"And so…we need your help. When you return to your countries, cities and towns, be ever diligent for signs of the Vagaries movements. Report back with anything suspicious, no matter how small. You never know what you might uncover." Vivica motions to Grace and she crosses the room to stand beside her.

"This is Grace Bennet. She, along with her Kindred from the future, were able to successfully open the portals." Vivica nods, and Grace pulls the Ambitus from the pocket of the sweater. The emerald sparkles on the dagger hilt, reflecting off the chandelier overhead.

"At the last house meeting, we were searching for this, the second Ambitus. Grace found it in Egypt. She activated it, unaware of its power. This set in motion a chain of events that led to the portals opening. We are very grateful to the brave Kairos who fought the Vagaries and would like to acknowledge them at this time."

Grace grins, her eyes meeting mine and motions me forward. I hesitate. So much for staying back and watching quietly.

Avery grabs my arm and drags me forward with her to stand beside Grace. Trina and Raymond join us from where they'd been sitting on a sofa beside Matthew and Scarlet. Clara briefly pats my arm then faces the room.

The Kairos begin to clap and heat creeps up my neck. I don't want praise or applause. I don't want thanks or recognition. I want revenge. Seven of us arrived in that portal. A pitifully small number compared to the Vagaries that ruled our world.

Quinton steps forward and lifts a hand until the applause subsides.

"Thank you for your service to mankind, Kindred," he

says. "We've won this battle, yes, but the war rages on. Let us remain diligent until the end. We will begin our quest by first keeping our eyes and ears open. Thank you for your time and God speed."

Numerous Kindred come forward to offer their fealty. I shake hands with dozens of Kairos, whose names I will never remember. The pretty Spanish girl I had noticed earlier is talking to Alejandro, and I cross the room to stand beside them.

"Hey, there you are. This is Christian, one of the Kairos from our time," Alejandro says.

"I'm Elena Perez. I'm happy to make your acquaintance," she replies. "I'm extremely interested at the prospect of traveling through time like this. It opens up so many possibilities." She smiles brightly at Alejandro.

"Let me get you something to drink and I'll tell you more about it," Alejandro says, chest puffing out a bit. They cross to a table in the back where Juanita has placed drinks and small sandwiches on silver trays.

I realize they are speaking Spanish, but for some reason I can understand them completely. I have picked up a few words throughout the years, but I could never understand a full sentence. I shrug inwardly and decide it was probably just a fluke.

My stomach rumbles. I could do with some food also and as I'm making my way to the back, pass several people conversing in other languages.

"We are cautiously optimistic. The battle with the Vagaries is far from over and now we have this new opportunity," says a tall man. His trim bushy eyebrows come together in a V over his prominent nose. I guess he's speaking Russian from the sharp accented words... a language that I normally wouldn't understand. Today, surprisingly, I understand every word he says. I shake my head. Something strange is going on here.

Food forgotten, I meander through the crowd. Everywhere I go, I understand what is being said, no matter the language spoken. Am I the only one who has this new ability?

Avery catches my eye. She nods, shakes an eager young man's hand and makes her way to me. She leans close and whispers in my ear.

"That German guy asked me for a date. I pretended like I couldn't understand his accent, you know, so I wouldn't hurt his feelings. Then he spoke to me in German." Her eyes grow round, "Christian, I totally understood everything he said! Isn't that strange?"

"It happened to me, too. Come on," I say. Avery slips her hand in mine and we make our way to Clara and Grace.

"Can we talk in private?" I ask. Clara nods, but when she sees my face, she frowns.

"Is something wrong?"

"I'm not sure yet. Maybe somethings right," I say. After all the heartache and trouble we've gone through, we would all welcome some good news.

Vivica and Quinton are busy with their guests so we slip away quietly and enter the study at the front of the house. Dante accompanies Grace, his hand on her arm as they stand beside Clara. I push down a tinge of annoyance and remind myself that he's on our side.

I explain to Clara and Grace what was happening with languages.

"It's quite exciting. I hope this ability is permanent. It will be so great for our assignments," Avery says.

"The house meeting was a success, don't you think?" Dante says, in a foreign language. "Do you understand what I'm saying? I'm speaking Italian."

Avery and I glance at each other nodding. "Yes, we understand you," she says.

"You spoke in Italian and said the house party was a success," I add.

"Wait. I understood you, too," Grace says in amazement. "How did this happen?" She thinks for a moment.

"Could it have something to do with opening the portal? We were all in it together, except you, Dante."

"I was speaking to several Kindred before the meeting and I didn't have this ability you're talking about. It must be just those of you who were present when the portal was opened," Dante replies.

"I haven't been around many people since I arrived," Clara says. She glances briefly at Grace and then says, "Let's talk with the others and find out."

We head back to the great room and the house meeting. There are many people I have yet to meet. I've always been more of a loner and it's strange to know there are so many travelers in the world.

My head spins as I'm introduced to more Kairos. I wonder what will happen next.

FIVE

GRACE

I lie in bed and stare at the dark ceiling. A cot was moved into Scarlets room for me. It's only been a few days, but they have been filled with planning and worry. I've trained with Quinton daily and Liam insisted I have another go at target practice. I still hate guns, but I can see the value in this situation, although I don't know if I could actually shoot anyone. I hope I never have to find out.

I haven't had an opportunity to talk more with Clara as she has been sticking close to Vivica. The weather has been warmer the past few days and Mom and Henry have been hanging out in the back gardens. Mom reads with him every day and he's been keeping up with his school work.

The Kairos continue to watch for the Vagaries to make a

move, but it's as if they've gone underground. Castillo hasn't been seen since I arrived in New York City, although I know he's here. He tried to get to me through Mom.

I touch the cool metal of the Ambitus where it lays beside my pillow. Vivica locked up the other artifacts in her safe, insisting that they were priceless. Vivica wanted the Ambitus also, but I kept it with me. What good would it be locked away, especially as it only responds to me? The tasks ahead weigh heavy on my heart tonight, along with an unknown future. Xavier Castillo knows we have the Ambitus and Excalibur. I'm not sure if he knows about the Flag or the Challis. I hope not. We need to keep some things to ourselves if we hope to prevail.

"Can't sleep?" Scarlet whispers from the darkness.

"No," I sigh, and turn to face her.

I need to talk to someone about all this. The artifacts, Xavier, my mother and Clara. It's all a jumble in my brain, circling like horses on a merry-go-round. I miss Jillian something fierce, also. I haven't had a chance to see her yet. She's my best friend and I'm used to confiding everything to her. I can't do that now, of course. It's too dangerous. Jacob said he'd bring her to visit me tomorrow afternoon, though. At least I have that to look forward to.

"Ever since I've joined the Kairos, it's been one thing after another," I say.

"I know how you feel. Sometimes it's overwhelming. That's why we have to lean on each other."

"I don't know why I was chosen by the Ambitus. Was it because I'm a Kairos and happened upon it, or is it something more?" I ask.

"I don't have the answers, Grace. Life has a way of putting us through unexpected challenges. It's up to us how we respond. I was younger than you when I joined the Kairos. It took me quite a while to adjust to my new reality."

"Everything happened so fast," I admit. "One day I was a normal high school senior looking forward to graduation and then suddenly I'm a Kairos fighting Marco and the Vagaries." I smooth a hand over the soft, cool sheets, and sigh. I've never really talked about Marco and the day he died. There wasn't time. Only a day later I was transported into the future with Clara.

"I didn't mean to kill him, Scarlet. Marco was chasing me and wanted the Ambitus. I knew he could easily take it from me. I just wanted to stop him. The dagger had other ideas, I guess. It flew out of my hand as if it had its target in sight and that was it. Marco was dead." I shudder as I remember the terrifying events of that day.

"You did what you had to do," Scarlet says.

I swallow back the lump in my throat and bury my head in the pillow, breathing in the fresh scent of the linens. I'm back home in New York City now. I'm with Dante again. My mom and little brother are safe in Kairos house, I remind myself.

"Try to get some rest. We have a big day ahead of us

tomorrow. We will be patrolling the streets for Vagary activity. Vivica wants to try and lure the Vagaries out of hiding. We need to be aware of any movement in the city."

"Thanks, Scarlet," I whisper.

I roll onto my back and gaze out of the window. Tomorrow would normally be a school day for me. I can't go back now. I know I'll have to deal with school at some point, but for now I'm to be tutored at Kairos house.

The clouds part and the moon sends a sliver of light across the bed. The Ambitus gleams once more, and I close my eyes. Scarlets right. I should be asleep. Instead, I replay the moment when I held up Excalibur joining all the knives together, the Flag of Macleod around my shoulders, the Challis, filled with Christians blood, clasped in my hand. I marvel at the memory but can't help the tremble that courses through me. Clutching the pillow tightly to my chest I close my eyes and wonder what will happen next.

SIX

CHRISTIAN

I walk down the streets of Manhattan trying not to look like a tourist, but I can't help gazing around me at the city. Its' skyscrapers are massive and there are so many people. The streets are full of them, hurrying to their various destination, oblivious to the drama between the Kairos and Vagaries unfolding around them. I feel awkward and out of place here.

A middle aged Asian woman pushes a cart, selling pot stickers, fried rice and other dishes. She's intent on her customers and doesn't notice us as we pass. I swallow uncomfortably and look away. She is a painful reminder to me of the people we left behind in Missouri struggling to make it one day at a time.

We'd split into several groups after breakfast. When I was

assigned to the group with Grace, Dante, Jacob and Matthew, the knot in my shoulders eased a bit. Grace had protested that she didn't need four guys to protect her, but that was the only way Vivica would allow her to leave the confines of Kairos house and venture out into the city. Grace had pointed out that she needed to be seen to draw out the Vagaries.

"That's the Brooklyn bridge," Grace says, moving to my side and pointing to the cable and stone structure we're about to cross. "It spans the east river connecting Brooklyn and Manhattan,"

"It's the oldest bridge in the city, built in 1833," Jacob says.

"Dante and I have had several scuffles with Vagaries on this bridge over the years," Matthew adds, a far-off look in his eye.

Dante pats him on the back and mummers, "Good times, mate."

They laugh and move forward, stepping onto the bridge. We traipse along the sidewalk as six lanes of cars zoom past. I don't like this. The vehicles travel too close and at high speeds. Even though Grace's hand is clasped firmly in Dante's, I move to walk between her and the road, blocking her from the speeding vehicles. Bicyclists and pedestrians share the sidewalk with us and I scan every face; which is kind of pointless since I don't know any of the Vagaries in this city, except for Castillo.

It's a mild spring day, but the wind has picked up. I slide my hand deeper into my jacket pocket, fingering the cool handle of the switch blade I have hidden there. I have another blade in my boot. Matthew is armed with a 9mm Glock. It is somewhat reassuring that he carries heat.

It takes about ten minutes to cross to the other side of the bridge and I release a breath as we step onto the crosswalk. I don't like being exposed like that. We cross East River Drive and turn onto St James Place.

"We can usually find a few Vagaries around here," Jacob says, rubbing his hands together. He moves smoothly on the balls of his feet, ready for a fight. We walk for several more minutes without speaking. I feel the begins of a headache tighten my neck and flex my shoulders. It will take time to get used to the car horns and traffic sounds that assault my ears. We continue to walk for several blocks with no sign of the Vagaries.

The streets are mostly clear of pedestrians in this area. We turn a corner and I notice two men, one about my age and one older with silver at his temples, exit a building a block ahead. One of them looks our way and says something to his companion. They turn to face us. The older man pulls open a long trench coat to reveal a wicked looking sword at his side. These are the first Vagaries I've seen since coming to New York. I still despise them.

We out number them, five to two. I'm feeling pretty confident until two more guys exit the building and join their friends on the sidewalk. Crap. I glance at Grace, but Dante and Jacob have closed ranks, positioning themselves in front of her. Matthew moves in time with my steps as we advance on the enemy, stopping about ten feet away.

"Hello, Paulo. I haven't seen you around New York in a while," Matthew says, gesturing to the older guy with the sword. Matthew stands with his feet apart and shoulders back. With his height and bulk, he's an imposing figure.

"What rock did you crawl out from under?" he drawls, his voice cold.

Paulo shrugs as if Matthews insult doesn't faze him, but his lips thin in his angular, hawk-like face.

"We have a message for Grace," Paulo says in a soft Latin accent. "Xavier wants to talk to her, a friendly gesture, between family, you know."

The Vagaries all nod in agreement. We don't move. No one buys his *friendly* gesture. Paulo drops the pretense along with the false smile.

"I think Vivica might have something to say about that. Castillo should meet with her first; go through the proper channels," Jacob says stiffly.

Paulo narrows his eyes, a sneer crossing his sharp features. "If the Kairos can't be…civil, then we might have to resort to more drastic measures." He rests his hand on the sword once more.

I tense, my hands balling into fists. I'm ready to step forward and plant my fist in this Paulo guy's face. Grace slips past Dante and grabs my arm, stopping me. She's learned to read me pretty well in the last few months.

"It's okay. Let me handle this," she whispers, then turns to face the Vagaries.

"I'll talk to Vivica," Grace says, taking one small step forward. "My family is the Kairos. Castillo knows this. Perhaps we can meet at an agreed upon location. I won't come alone, though. You can tell him that."

Paulo shrugs, then the Vagaries back up a few steps before turning and disappearing around the corner. I can't imagine what Grace is thinking. She knows she can't trust Castillo.

"You aren't seriously going to meet him?" I say, incredulous.

"I don't know," she says with a sigh. "I had to say something."

"Paulo is part of the Brazilian Vagaries. If he is in New York, I assume Castillo has called more Vagaries to New York and this fight is about to escalate," Dante says. "Let's see what Vivica says." He turns to Grace, his face troubled. "Whatever happens, I'm going with you. I won't risk losing you again."

"We should return to Kairos house immediately. Vivica will want to know of this development right away," Matthew says. He slips his phone from his pocket and calls Bruce to bring a car around to pick us up. We walk to the end of the street to wait.

The breeze loosens a few strands of Grace's hair from where she's pulled it back in a braid. Dante tucks it behind her ear and she smiles into his eyes.

I turn away quickly and watch a piece of newspaper blow down the street. I remind myself once again that I have to let her go, but it's a hard habit to break.

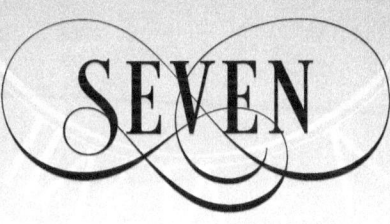

SEVEN

GRACE

The guys circle around me like I'm about to be kidnapped at any moment. It's annoying, yet oddly touching, how protective they are. Luckily, it only takes Bruce a few minutes from the time he received Matthews call to arrive at our location. Driving quickly, we return to Kairos house within minutes. Juanita ushers us inside. We follow her into the great room.

"I'll be right back with coffee," she says, bustling out of the room, muttering under her breath in Spanish.

"These young people never eat enough," she whispers as if her food is the answer to everything.

"I'll cook my Italian dinner tonight. That should fill them up, and of course a nice flan to go with it," she mutters to herself, closing the door behind her. I turn to Dante with startled eyes, remembering the new ability with language we discovered last night. Evidently it's still working. Vivica and Quinton enter the room and turn my attention to the problem at hand.

"That didn't take long," Vivica says, sitting on a chair and crossing her legs delicately. Quinton stands behind her, his arm on the back of her chair, supporting her in his quiet way. "I suppose they were expecting you."

"Probably. They had a message from Castillo. He wants to talk to Grace," Dante says.

"Absolutely not," Vivica replies, calmly leaning back in her chair and folding her arms. "He must know I would never agree to such a thing."

"Of course not. But perhaps we can arrange a meeting at Battery Park. We've used the park as neutral territory in the past," Dante says.

"How is the park neutral territory?" I ask. This is the first I've heard of such a thing.

"Battery Park is close to the ocean. There are no portals within a half mile of any shoreline. It protects us from ending up underwater when we travel," Dante says.

I nod. It makes sense, I guess. I learn new things about the Kairos every day.

"The park is a popular place, though. Won't it be crowded with people?" I ask.

"It won't be busy if we go at first light. We might encounter a jogger or two, but they usually ignore us," Dante replies.

The door opens and Scarlet rushes into the room along with Elena, the pretty Spanish girl I met at the house party. Liam and Trina follow behind them.

"What happened?" Scarlet says, breathlessly. "Matthew texted that you made contact with the Vagaries."

I pat the spot beside me on the sofa and Scarlet sits down, turning to me.

"Castillo wants to talk to me," I say. "I'm think he's hoping to get answers as to how we opened the portals."

"You're not going to meet with him, are you? It will be a trap," Scarlet says.

"I won't go alone, no. But I think a group of us should see what he has to say."

"He wants you, obviously. You have abilities he wants to exploit. You need to stay at Kairos house, away from Castillo," Dante says, firmly.

"I can't just hide here for the rest of my life," I protest, turning to Dante. "I'm sure with the protection of the Kairos, I'll be fine. Safety in numbers, right?"

Dante frowns, unconvinced. I know he's worried. I am too, but we need to find out what Castillo is after and eliminate the threat as quickly as possible so my family can get back to their lives.

"I'll see if I can arrange a meeting tomorrow morning in

Battery Park with Castillo. I'll tell him Grace will be there, but only if she has protection," Liam says.

Dante squeezes my hand gently, reassuring me that he will watch out for me. I let out a long breath. It's not like I *want* to talk to Xavier Castillo, but knowing he's my Great Uncle has me a bit curious. How do I fit in to the whole battle between good and evil, Kairos and Vagary? After all, I'm a part of both of them.

I find Mom and Henry in the study. Henry is sitting at the desk working on some math problems. He narrows his eyes in concentration. Mom sits next to him.

"Remember to carry over this number," she says, pointing with a pencil to the paper. I close the door behind me and cross the room to peer over Henry's shoulder.

"How are you guy's doing?" I ask.

"I don't like math that much, but I get to do archery with Quinton after I finish," Henry says. "He has a bow my size and everything."

"That'll be fun. Quinton's a great instructor," I say, ruffling Henry's hair. I'm grateful that the Kairos have been so kind to my family. Having an energetic boy underfoot must take some getting used to for a house full of adults.

Henry returns to his math problem, his tongue sticking out

of the side of his mouth as he works. Mom rises and we leave the room and into the grand foyer, away from curious ears.

"How was patrol?" she asks quietly, her eyes searching mine.

"We were successful. We made contact with the Vagaries. That's what I wanted to talk to you about."

Mom grips my arm. "Go on."

I tell her about our plans. I hold up a hand as she begins to protest.

"We need to know what their objective is at this point. Don't worry, this is no way I'll meet him alone. Vivica is going to try to work out a meeting with him at a neutral place."

"I don't understand what goes into this time-travel business, but I don't like this, Grace. I don't think you should be leaving Kairos house. I'm worried about you. I just want you to be safe."

"I know. Don't worry, I'll be careful. The Kairos are trained and are excellent body guards." I say, trying to reassure her. Mom slips her arm around me and I lay my head on her shoulder. The smell of her floral perfume surrounds me as I gaze through the window at the fountain of Atlas, the world on his shoulders. No wonder I'm drawn to the statue. It feels like everyone is depending on me to somehow fix this mess.

EIGHT

CHRISTIAN

I ease the barbell to the floor and grab a towel, wiping the sweat from my forehead. I've managed to pass the afternoon lifting weights, but now the tantalizing smell of garlic bread and tangy baked cheese wafts through the house, reaching me even down in the basement and my stomach growls in anticipation. I ignore it.

Vivica contacted the Vagary leader to arrange a meeting. Now we wait for a reply. It's surreal to be here, in New York City, and I tell myself it will take a some time to adjust. I can't get the woman I saw this morning out of my mind., though. She reminded me of my mother. After escaping the Vagaries, I tried to find her without success and have no idea where she is now, or even of she's alive. Memories of her baking bread with the little bit of flour she was able to save, and her selling her goods on the street as she had no other way to provide for us.

I cross to the punching bag hanging in the corner and take a satisfying swing, connecting with more force than necessary. I transfer my frustrations to my fists, the bag absorbing the blows. This is what I'm really fighting for… the people I left behind and the uncertain future they face; one that I hope will become a little easier because of my actions.

The door opens and Trina and Avery appear.

"There you are. I'm supposed to tell you dinner is in fifteen minutes," Avery says. She wrinkles her nose at my sweaty t-shirt. "You probably should shower first, though."

"What? You don't like the way I smell? Come on, give me a hug," I tease and pretend to reach for her." Avery dances away laughing.

"Don't come any closer," she says, hands up.

"Okay, okay. I guess I'll take a quick shower first," I say, with a shrug.

I'd planned on showering anyway, but Avery can be annoyingly bossy sometimes. Trina wanders over to the shelves holding the weapons.

"I've always wanted to learn to fight with one of these," she says, running her hand down the smooth surface of a quarterstaff pole. It looks lethal, with metal spikes on each end.

"Later," Avery says, pulling her out of the room. "I'm starving. All this training and battle talk has made me hungry."

47

The girls leave, shutting the door behind them. I shower quickly and dress in a pair of jeans and a clean t-shirt, and climb the stairs to the main floor. I follow my nose to the kitchen.

Juanita has expanded the wooden table, now covered in a red and white checked cloth, to fit the large groups of Kairos. It's laden with loaves of chunky garlic bread and a huge bowl of salad. I take the empty seat next to Alejandro. Matthew plops down next to me.

"Where is everyone else?" I ask.

"Vivica and Quinton don't eat with us. They'll be in the formal dining room, usually entertaining guests," Matthew says, holding up his hand, pinky extended, like royalty drinking tea. Scarlet punches his arm and he laughs.

"You know they take their responsibilities seriously," she says, scolding.

"Just joking, sis," Matthew says with a laugh.

Jacob throws an arm around Scarlet and shakes his head. "Never tease a hungry woman."

Scarlet punches him, too and he yelps, rubbing his arms. These Kairos are obviously close friends. I smile slightly at their antics and feel slightly out of place.

I notice Grace, Dante, Clara, and Raymond aren't in the kitchen either. I guess they'll be eating with Vivica and Quinton, also.

Juanita places a steaming pan of lasagna in the middle of the table. She plops a huge slice in the middle of my plate.

"You look hungry. You need to eat more, build up your strength," she says, patting my arm. She nods, and continues to serve everyone else.

She's probably right. I could stand to gain a few pounds. Food hasn't been as important as survival in the last few weeks. Everyone is silent for a few minutes as we dig into the meal. Jacob takes a drink of water and then clears his throat.

"I wanted to warn the new Kairos about the Vagaries here in New York," he says. "As you know, travelers are extremely rare and the Vagaries like to try and recruit new Kairos to join them. If they make contact with any of you, please come to me and let me know."

I raise an eyebrow and glance at Alejandro. He shrugs, looking down at his plate. None of our group would *ever* consider joining the Vagaries. I guess Jacob doesn't know us, though. He doesn't know what we've lived through at the Vagaries hands. After an awkward silence, I say,

"You don't have to worry about any of us. We may be new to New York, but we are very aware of the treachery of our enemy."

"True that," Avery adds, nodding and crossing her arms over her chest.

"Please don't take offense," Jacob says, raising a hand. "I'm not accusing you of anything. It's just a warning that we share with any new Kairos."

"Alright. Message received," I say. I doubt any Vagary

connected to Xavier Castillo will be approaching us. They know we stand firmly with the Kairos.

I've just finished the second helping of the Flan dessert that Juanita insisted on serving me, when Dante and Grace enter the kitchen.

"We've received word from Castillo. We'll meet tomorrow morning at dawn in Battery Park."

"I don't know why we have to meet with Castillo at all. Couldn't we just…ignore him? I mean, what are we trying to accomplish?" Trina asks. She wrinkles her nose in distaste. I understand her reluctance. Trina has reason to hate Castillo. He kidnapped and molested her. He would have done worse if Grace and I hadn't found her in time.

"This accomplishes several of our objectives. We want to force his hand, putting him on the defensive. We can see who he has with him and hopefully get an idea of what he plans to do next," Dante says.

"He wants Grace. I think that's obvious," I say, flatly, glancing I her direction. "I don't think Grace should go anywhere near that meeting."

"I have to go. I've already said I'd be there. Don't worry, Christian. I'll have you all as protection." Grace says, gesturing at the room full of her kindred.

I want to object, but instead I nod. I have no right to make decisions for Grace. I can't help the worry that creeps across my chest and settles in the pit of my stomach, though. We don't know what we're walking into. We'll be armed and prepared, but so will the Vagaries.

I thank Juanita for the delicious meal, and she smiles brightly, her cheeks pink with pleasure at the praise. We file from the kitchen, and everyone disperses to their different assignments. Mine is to train with the other Kairos in hand to hand combat. That is a task I'll gladly accept. Physical exercise is always welcome and maybe it will help take my mind off of tomorrow's meeting with Castillo.

NINE

GRACE

I stand in the foyer of Kairos house, tapping my foot impatiently. Jacob is on his way with Jillian and I'm beyond excited to see my best friend. I realize that for her we've only been apart for a few days, but for me it's been months. I know I look the same but I feel totally different. So much has happened in that time.

Vivica softened her stance and is allowing Jillian inside Kairos house since she covered for me when I disappeared.

"Hi, Grace," he says, scurrying down the stairs, a box of LEGO's in his arms. He stops beside me, his eyes clear and bright, and I steal a hug before he wiggles free.

"Going to build something fun?" I ask, peering over his shoulder.

"Yeah, A medieval castle, with a tower and moat and everything," he exclaims.

"Looks amazing."

Henry nods, his eyes glued to the box and skips away happily to the back of the house.

I shake my head. Vivica's had to do even more softening now that Mom and Henry are living in Kairos house.

I'm startled when the door behind me opens and Jacob and Jillian enter the foyer.

"Grace!" Jillian squeals. She rushes forward and hugs me tightly. "Oh my gosh, you totally freaked me out! Don't ever do that again."

I nod, and grin at Jillian. She looks amazing in skinny jeans and a black silk top, her blonde locks framing her gorgeous face. I glance at Jacob and ask,

"How did you get here? Did you travel?"

"Yes, I thought it might be easier that way. We know the house is being watched." He shrugs like it's no big deal, but I can see the tension in his eyes and the tight set of his jaw. Vivica rarely allows use of the portal inside the house for security reasons. They must really be worried, I think.

"Well, I'm just glad you're here. I've missed you terribly," I say, hugging Jillian again. She glances around the foyer her mouth forming a little 'oh' as she takes in the grandeur of the space.

"Oh. My. Gosh," she says, "this place is spectacular." I

laugh and take her hand.

"I'm stealing her away for a minute," I tell Jacob and he nods.

"Let's go to my room."

"You have your own room here?" Jillian asks, her eyes growing even rounder if that's possible.

"Well, no, not my own. I'm sharing with Scarlet, but we can talk privately there," I say as we ascend the staircase.

We climb slowly while Jillian gazes at the fine art on the walls. She stops to admire a lovely bronze statue of a roman gladiator, spear at the ready, which is displayed in a niche in the wall.

"Daddy would die to see all this," she breathes. I nod in agreement and we continue up the stairs. He probably would love a tour of Kairos house as her dads an antiquities dealer.

We've just reached the landing at the top when Christian emerges from the basement into the foyer below us. He's dressed in workout gear, his broad shoulders and bulging arm muscles glistening with sweat. He doesn't notice us standing at the top of the stairs and crosses the hall to disappear into the great room. He's gorgeous, as always. I sigh. He was also my best friend while I was in Missouri and it's been an adjustment for both of us, retuning to Kairos house.

"Who was that?" Jillian asks, fanning herself. I smile and pull her down the hall to my room.

Once inside, we sit on the sofa by the window.

"That's Christian. He's a Kairos from the future. He helped me immensely when I was trying to figure out how to get back here. He's a good friend," I say. My words don't really begin to express my relationship with Christian. It's different than the connection I have with Dante, but real none the less.

"Well, he's gorgeous. Not as handsome as Jacob, but still. Wow. How do you manage to find all these dreamy guys?"

"I think it's just being around the Kairos. They are just naturally attractive."

"Tell me about it," Jillian sighs. "You're positively glowing too, Grace. Whatever you've been doing, it's working for you." She grins.

"Did Jacob tell you what happened to me?"

"Only that you were stuck in the future. He was *so* worried about you. I was so relieved when he told me you made it back."

I nod. Relief is just one of the emotions I feel right now. Hopeful, grateful, worried and anxious, all rolled into one. No wonder I couldn't sleep last night.

"Thank you for covering for me with Mom. She knows all about it now, but I'm glad she wasn't aware of what was really going on at the time. She would have been frantic."

Jillian nods, gazing around the beautiful bedroom. She turns to me, face suddenly serious. "Promise me you won't do anything crazy in your battle with the bad guys." She waves her arm, "I know you have been training to fight and all that, but it freaks me out. You're my best friend. I want you around, you know? "

"I *want* to be around, believe me," I say. "I found out something crazy while I was gone, also."

I tell her that Clara is my biological mother and how she hid me with her sister to protect me. She rubs my arm. "Oh my gosh, Grace. That's a lot to take in. Are you okay?"

I nod, and manage a crocked smile.

"So you're like some kind of weird, super hybrid, crossbreed time-traveler?" she asks, her eyes wide. "That's *so* cool."

"I don't know what I am," I say, shaking my head. "This is all new to me, too."

Jillian grabs me in a hug. "You be safe, Grace Bennet, you hear me. I don't want to lose you again," she whispers.

I nod, retuning the hug. "I'll do my best," I say.

I'm new at all of this Kairos business, but the enemy has been around for centuries. I cross my fingers and pray my best is good enough.

TEN

CHRISTIAN

I stand in the foyer of Kairos house and adjust the strap of the sword and sheath attached to my back, making sure I have quick access. I swear Alejandro has stashed ten knives about his person. Elena Perez, the Spanish girl from the meeting last night looks like some super woman in black leather pants and a heavy mesh top covered by a leather vest. Alejandro can't take his eyes off of her as she slips a knife in each boot and a crossbow over her shoulder. She looks lethal.

Grace is dressed simply in a pair of jeans and a camo army jacket. The Ambitus she carries in her pocket is the only weapon she brings. I've seen that thing in action and know how deadly it can be. Vivica was concerned about bringing such a priceless artifact within reach of Castillo, but Grace insisted. She won't go anywhere without it.

A pair of brass knuckles and several blades are all I take today. Regardless of what Dante or anyone else does, my main purpose is to protect Grace. I asked Liam if he plans on carrying a firearm, but he said guns attract too much attention in the park, so we stick to more traditional weapons. I have no idea what will happen this morning. I only know I don't trust Castillo one bit.

Scarlet, Matthew, Liam and Trina are ready. Scarlet looks calm, except for the way she bounces on the toes. Jacob and Dante enter the foyer followed by Quinton and Vivica, Raymond and Clara. About ten more Kairos from last night join us. We number about twenty five Kindred. We'll fight in teams, back to back, as Quinton assigned. I'll fight along-side Matthew, but my eyes will be on Grace.

I glance at the clock on the entry table. 5:15 am. The sun will rise in about an hour and we need to be in position. Kairos house is just over a mile to Battery Park so we'll walk the twenty minutes instead of worrying about transportation. Bruce opens the front door, Juanita by his side.

"If you need the car, I'll be waiting," he tells Vivica.

"Thank you, Bruce," she nods, adjusting the sword at her hip and stepping outside.

Juanita makes the sign of the cross and kisses her rosary beads neckless as we pass into the courtyard. The cool morning is refreshing and I take a deep breath and rotate my shoulders.

I'm ready for whatever Castillo brings. We move past the fountain, through the gates and onto the street.

Liam, Vivica and Quinton take the lead. I trail Grace and Dante, while Matthew and Scarlet walk beside me. I glance around. It's still dark on the street and I don't like being out in the open like this.

We cross the road to avoid a particularly bright street light. Vivica chooses a less direct route to avoid any traffic. We walk quickly down Varick Street toward Broadway and Lower Manhattan. We move fast, a group of heavily armed Kairos, intent upon our mission.

When we arrive at the park, the security team led by Liam, breaks away and enters first. They will spread out and take their assigned positions, on the lookout for any Vagary tricks. The large group of trees, called the Battery Woodland, is our destination. I studied the map earlier and thought I was familiar with the parks amenities, but it is much larger than I had imagined. I glance around nervously. There are too many places for an ambush. Time seems to crawl by and I shift from one foot to the other almost expecting the Vagaries to jump out of the trees and attack. The beauty of the surroundings is marred by what is about to come.

The sun is just beginning to filter through the trees when Xavier Castillo, tall and powerfully built, his dark hair smoothed back from his forehead, strolls into the Woodlands area. He's accompanied by about twenty Vagaries. Castillo is tall and good looking with dark hair and an angular face. The Vagaries are well armed also, the swell of weapons visible beneath their clothing. I move closer to Grace, ready to pull my knife if necessary.

"My, aren't we civilized," Castillo drawls, his arms folded across his chest. "Grace, dear, you're looking well, after all the drama you created when last we met."

"You may address me," Vivica says regally, stepping in front of Grace.

"As much as I'd love to chat and catch up, Vivica, I came to talk to my Great Niece," Castillo says. He steps forward and two hulking body guards move with him. One is as big as Liam with powerful arms and a thick neck. The other is slim, but strong, with hard eyes that take in our numbers.

"It's alright," Grace says to Vivica and faces Castillo.

"What did you want to talk about? I assume it's not my mother, Linda, as you've already met her," Grace says, eyes narrowing.

"Lovely, woman, your mother. It's too bad she didn't have any of your abilities, but I had to find out for myself, you understand." His smile doesn't quite reach his eyes.

Grace stiffens and Dante moves closer.

"Leave my mother alone. She has nothing to do with any of this," Grace says.

"Let's leave Grace out of this, too, Castillo." Clara says stiffly, standing close to Grace.

"Ah, another mama bear to the rescue. How charming," Castillo drawls, his dislike palpable on his angular face. "Haven't you caused enough trouble for everyone? We have the right to get to know Grace. She should be with us, along with the Ambitus, of course. You've had your chance, Vivica, now it's our turn. Consider it… joint custody."

"Stop this," Grace says fiercely, interrupting Castillo, her hands on hips. "I'm not a child to be fought over."

"No?" Castillo drawls, "but your abilities might be worth the battle. Isn't that right, Vivica? Isn't that *really* why you want Grace all to yourself? Not because she's family, but because you want to use her for your own purposes."

Vivica's hand goes to the sword at her waist and Castillo laughs.

"Come now, Vivica. You, of all people, should appreciate plain speaking. We are in a unique time in our history. The portals of the world are finally open to us. We have a rare opportunity before us. Don't waste it. Let us join together and take our rightful place, leading the world to its destiny."

"Never. Your ways are not the Kairos. We are fundamentally different. We will never turn over the fate of this world to you," Vivica says, scornfully.

"Ah well. I was afraid you would say that. Such a shame, really." Castillo nods slowly then steps back, raising his fist in the air, his security detail closing rank around him. The Vagaries fan out, drawing their weapons. So much for neutral territory.

I pull my sword and step in front of Grace, Matthew by my side. Dante takes Grace's other side. Dante and I glance at each other and nod. We won't let anything happen to her.

The other Kairos move into fighting teams, weapons drawn, ready for battle. An arrow flies by my head and I duck down as the Vagaries attack.

The clang of metal on metal breaks through the quiet morning. Matthew, Dante and I form a secure perimeter around Grace.

Clara kicks one Vagary, knocking his legs out from under him, Vivica finishes him with her sword just as another two run toward them. Matthew and I take on two that are trying to get to Grace. While I hold off a large Vagaries sword, Matthew takes a more direct route and punches the guy in the face, the powerful blow knocking him on his back. Elena's arrow hits the downed Vagary in the shoulder effectively taking him out of the fight.

Trina and Avery face off with two Vagary girls. Avery and Trina's karate moves are impressive, especially as they have had years to perfect fighting together. Avery lands a kick to a dark haired girls face, and she falls on her back, blood spurting from her mouth. Liam fights two Vagaries at once, easily holding them off.

We are beginning to turn the battle in our favor, when the fight is interrupted by a piercing scream and loud barking. A jogger and her dog have entered the Woodland area and stumbled upon us. She's on the phone, her dog straining at the leash. Thank God she isn't live streaming this, or we'd be in deep trouble, not to mention the evening news. It won't be long before the police arrive though. We can't risk exposure. The fighting immediately slows.

I quickly take stock of the Kairos. Raymond has a knife wound on his arm and Alejandro a bloody nose and lip, but other than that we are fine. The Vagaries fared far worse. Several of their numbers are dead with at least five injured.

Dante ushers Grace out of the park, along with Vivica and Clara. I watch as the Vagaries gather up their dead and wounded and retreat back the way they came. I linger for a few moments to make sure all of our Kindred are accounted for and have left the area before I take up the rear.

Suddenly an arrow hits my shoulder from behind, knocking me to the ground. The sound of feet pounding behind me is followed by hands grabbing me. They pull my sword off my back. I struggle to free myself, but intense pain shoots through my shoulder. I'm dragged away from the open area, behind a group of thick trees.

"I had hoped for Grace, but you'll have to do," Castillo says, looking down at me. "Take him to the boat." He gestures to his bodyguards.

My hands are bound and I swear under my breath as I'm pulled to my feet. Damn. The arrow protrudes through my shoulder and feels like I have a hot poker pressed into it. Every movement is agony.

Their plan had been to kidnap Grace, I realize. When that failed, they settled on me. I don't have the abilities that Grace has, but they'll probably use me as bate to try and get to her. They should have grabbed Dante. I don't think they'll get anywhere with me. The thought doesn't make me feel very confident about my chance of survival.

The Vagaries slip under my arms, dragging me through the park and onto a dock where a speed boat is secured. There is no use calling out to the other Kairos. I don't want Grace coming back to look for me and they wouldn't hear me anyway.

I'm shoved to the floor of the boat. I land on my arm and try not to pass out from the pain. Blood stains the carpet of the deck beneath me as the boat takes off at high speed through the upper bay of the Atlantic ocean. I wish I was more familiar with the city. I have no idea where they are taking me.

I lay on my side and glaze at the passing clouds above me. The cold wind keeps me from passing out and the pain in my shoulder has lessened to a dull ache. I hope I don't have nerve damage. I need to get this arrow out of me as soon as possible.

Castillo nudges me with his boot. "Well now, we have a lot to talk about, don't we?"

I moan, hoping he'll think I'm in too much pain to talk. Hopefully, he'll remove the arrow, before infection sets in.

"We have excellent surgeons at our New Jersey headquarters. We'll take you there and get you fixed up. You'll see we aren't as bad as the Kairos have led you to believe."

A cold fist squeezes my chest as I think of the pain the Vagaries have caused my family in Missouri. I'll play along for a while, but I vow to escape. I just don't know how... yet.

ELEVEN

GRACE

We are barely out of the park when Matthew announces that Christian isn't with us.

"We have to go back and find him," I say, turning around quickly.

"You go with Dante and Vivica. The police will probably arrive soon. You shouldn't be here," Matthew says. He hands his sword to Liam. "Take this with you. I'll go find him."

"Won't you need a weapon?" I ask. He opens his coat to reveal the pistol strapped to his side.

The Ambitus trembles in my hand. Nothing can happen to Christian, I think. He's my Kindred, protector and friend. He *has* to be okay. I close my eyes and ask the Ambitus to show me where Christian is. Nothing happens at first, and I concentrate harder, trying to slow the pounding of my heart.

Suddenly, I see him as he comes into focus in my mind. He's lying on a beige carpet. I can't tell where he is, though. He has an arrow through his shoulder and blood pools beneath him. He's hurt.

"Wait. I see him," I say to Matthew. "He's not in the park anymore. I don't know where he is, but I can see that he's injured."

"I'll go back inside the park and see if I can find anything. You all get to the safety of Kairos house," Matthew says, his face pulled into a deep frown, his hands balled into fists. Matthew is a great friend, but a formidable enemy. I wouldn't want to be on the receiving end of his fury.

"I've already called Bruce to pick up Grace. He's on his way," Dante says, his arm sliding around me. I huddle into his warmth. I'm shaking with fear and worry. I feel so helpless, I could scream. This is all my fault. I should have never agreed to meet Castillo. I knew I couldn't trust him. I cover my face with my hands as a tear escapes. I swipe at my cheeks. Crying solves nothing. I'll use my tools to find Christian and get him back, I decide, firmly. I just have to come up with a plan, that's all.

Bruce pulls up to the curb just as the sound of sirens reaches my ears. The police are almost here. We need to be gone before they arrive.

Vivica, Quinton, Clara, Dante, and I pile into the Limo while the others take off jogging down a side street.

"Where would they be taking Christian?" I ask. "And why?"

"The Vagaries have properties in New York City, New Jersey, Los Angeles, Chicago, and Dallas, to name a few," Vivica says, shrugging. "He could be anywhere."

I sink lower in the seat, discouraged. How will we ever find him?

"We have properties in those cities also, plus many more. We are equipped to handle the situation. Castillo took him for a reason and I'm sure *you* are that reason, Grace" Vivica says, frowning. "When it became obvious he wouldn't be able to get to you he chose Christian instead."

"Well, he can't have Grace," Clara says, firmly. Her golden eyes blaze in conviction. I swallow and glance out of the window. I'm afraid what danger associating with me will bring to those I care about.

"Of course not," Vivica agrees, quickly. "I'm sure we'll have to concede something, or Castillo will never return Christian, otherwise. Castillo will leave him in some God forsaken place in history and we'll never find him."

I hadn't thought of that. I shake my head. I can't let that happen to Christian. He's been through too much already. I won't condemn him to that fate. My stomach drops to my toes as I suddenly wonder about other people who have gone missing. Are they stuck somewhere back in time, unable to get away? I have so many unanswered questions.

"I'm sure Castillo will send a demand soon. We'll decide

our next course of action at that time," Vivica says.

"So in the mean time we do nothing?" I ask, appalled. "Christian is injured. He could be in pain, or could be dying for all we know and we won't do anything I about it?"

"Try not to worry, my dear," Quinton says, "this kind of thing can happen when you're dealing with the Vagaries."

I shake my head. That doesn't make me feel any better. Dante takes my hand and squeezes it lightly.

"Christian's no good to Castillo dead. He'll probably travel with him, and allow the portal to heal him before he lets that happen," Dante adds.

I take a calming breath. Dante may be right, but it doesn't make me feel any better. We pull up to the front of Kairos house. Bruce jumps out and unlocks the gate. We scurry into the courtyard. Mom flings open the door and rushes outside.

"You're back safely. I'm so relieved," she says with a smile. She pulls me into an embrace and I hug her tightly. I'm lucky to have my mom, Henry, and Dante and Clara. Who does Christian have to worry about him, if not me? I step back and glance down the street. The rest of my Kindred have turned onto our block and are jogging toward Kairos house. My hand closes tightly around the Ambitus. I need a plan.

TWELVE

CHRISTIAN

It's cold in the basement where I've been locked up for God knows how long. It must be several hours. It has a musty, damp odor, and I shiver as the cold concrete floor offers little comfort. I'm thirsty, and my arm hurts like a bitch. Some guy, I don't know if he was a doctor or not, came down here a few hours ago. One of the Vagary girls from the battle this morning was with him. She's young, maybe sixteen or seventeen, with a riot of light brown curls around her face. She would have been pretty except for a fat lip and black eye, compliments of Avery. She stood to the side, hand on the dagger hanging from her belt and watched the Doc remove the arrow. It hurt so much I almost passed out. He gave me a shot in my butt cheek, which would have been slightly embarrassing, if I wasn't in too much pain to care. He said it was an antibiotic, bandaged my shoulder, and they both left. It was more than I expected, really. I figured they'd just let me die down here. The room is small and empty, save for one wooden chair and an ancient looking boiler.

Things could be worse. It could be Grace down here, lying on the floor injured. It's small consolation, I guess, but knowing her, she's already plotting some daring rescue. I hope Dante stops her from doing something foolish. I want her as far away from the Vagaries as possible. For some reason Castillo has kept me alive, and I'm hoping to use that to my advantage.

The door opens and footsteps stomp down the wooden stairs. The hulking bodyguard appears followed by Castillo. He pulls the lone chair over to where I lay and sits down, crossing his legs nonchalantly.

"So, now that you have been attended to, I have a few questions. Since you and Grace are such good friends, I'm sure you can answer them for me," he says, smiling like we're old friends having a friendly chat.

I shrug and try not to wince as pain shoots through my shoulder.

"I realize Grace has a natural talent with the Ambitus. I've seen her in action, after all. But what I want to know is how she opened all the portals. We haven't been able to do it since the fiasco with Clara years ago. She opened them for a brief period of time, but they quickly closed behind her. Occasionally, we might get lucky and find ourselves able to travel somewhere, but it's sporadic at best. As you know, this can also lead to catastrophe as a traveler can become trapped in a time-stop." He leans forward, staring at me intensely, then asks,

"How did Grace do it? How did she open the portals such that they remain open?"

"I need water," I croak through my dry throat, trying to buy time. I have no intension of telling him anything. Castillo motions to the hulking guard, who clomps back up the stairs. He returns a few minutes later with a bottle of water. I drink thirstily, emptying the bottle.

I stare at the ceiling, my arm throbbing in time to my rapidly pounding heart. I steal myself for some painful unpleasantness with the hulk. I know Castillo will not like my silence.

I say nothing. Castillo sighs as if his patience is wearing thin.

"Maybe I can jog your memory. I know she stole Excalibur from my office, but what else did she use?"

"Nothing," I say. "I don't know how she did any of it."

Castillo shakes his head. "Maybe you need a little assistance with your memory." He nods to the hulk, who crosses to me and punches me hard in the stomach. I gasp, and roll to my side, the wind knocked out of me.

"Now, let me ask one more time. What else did Grace use to open the portals?"

I shake my head and the hulk kicks me in the ribs. He grabs

my shirt and lifts me up, his arm pulled back ready to punch my face, when Castillo stops him.

"That's enough, Norm. Let's give our new friend time to think about his answers. I'm confident, when he weighs his options, his memory will return."

I lay gasping for breath, but all I can think is…Norm. The hulks name is Norm? I'd laugh if I could, but I can barely breathe. I prefer to think of him as hulk. I'm losing my mind. I've got to get out of here. I try to form an escape plan, but my brain is fuzzy with pain.

Castillo crosses to where I lay curled in a ball, fighting for breath. He squats down beside me and says quietly, "Don't be a hero, Christian; their blood is red and they die just like the rest of us." He stands and follows the hulk up the stairs.

THIRTEEN

GRACE

I pace the floor as the sun sinks beyond the horizon, throwing the bedroom into darkness. I can't just hide out in Kairos house and do nothing. I wring my hands and resume pacing. I have strict orders from Vivica to stay inside, but the thought of Christian hurt, and in the clutches of Castillo, has my stomach tied in knots. There has to be something I can do.

Scarlet enters the room and crosses to me, arm outstretched. I fall into them as she hugs me tight.

"I'm so sorry, Grace. I know Christian was a good friend of yours," she says, her eyes full of pity.

"Don't say that, like he's dead or something. I know he's still alive," I whisper, pulling out of her embrace.

"Come, sit down and talk to me," Scarlet says, leading me over to the settee by the window. She tucks a throw blanket around me like I'm a child. "Now, I'm sure you're right, but will you tell me how you know Christian is still alive."

"I guess I don't know it, but when I look for him with the Ambitus, I can see that he's still alive."

Scarlet nods, but looks a bit skeptical. I don't blame her. None of the occupants of Kairos house have seen what the Ambitus can do. I need to talk to Alejandro, or Avery, or Raymond. They will understand. I sigh and stare at the pretty pink rug. A sliver of an idea begins to form. Could I do it? Could I find Christian and free him? I know it's a big risk and Vivica would freak if she knew what I was considering. I'd have to use the Flag of Macleod, possibly the other artifacts too. The first problem…Vivica has them locked up in her safe. She'd never willingly give them to me. The second problem… using the artifacts to find Christian, I'd be playing right into the Vagaries hands. I'd be bringing the tools that control the portals right to them. I chew my lip, unsure what to do.

"What are you thinking?" Scarlet says, tilting her head to one side. "You look like you're planning something."

"Not really," I shrug, and fiddle with the edge of the blanket.

Scarlet pats my arm. "Let's go down to the gym and work off some of that frustration."

"Alright, just let me change," I agree. "I'm going mad doing nothing. Maybe some strength training is just what I need right now."

Maybe I'll see some of my Kindred, too. I need to think of some way to make this half formed plan work.

We quickly change into workout gear and make our way to the gym. It's almost 8 pm and the house is quiet. When we enter the gym I'm pleased to see Dante and Jacob already sparring. They're wearing boxing gloves and dance from side to side, trying to outmaneuver each other. I sigh, remembering how I learned to spar with Christian not too long ago.

Dante nods and grins at me. I smile back. He quickly focuses back on Jacob, jumping away from a punch that barely misses his head.

I cross to the barbells and adjust the weights. Scarlet follows and straps some exercise bands to her legs.

"Christian taught me a little bit about boxing," I say. "He's a skilled fighter and an asset to any team."

Am I being obvious, trying to sell Christian's abilities? I don't care, though. Surely, if I explain to Dante how I feel, he'll understand. If Jacob had been kidnapped by the Vagaries, Dante would be forming a rescue party right now.

"It a tough call, Grace. You need to trust Vivica to make the right decision. She's been the Kairos leader for a long time," Scarlet replies.

I shrug and lift the weights, but I can't really concentrate on the exercise. It's like the artifacts, locked in the safe upstairs, are calling my name. Maybe Vivica will allow me to visit them.

That sounds so silly, but that's how I feel.

"Can I adjust these for you?" Dante says, coming to stand beside me. He smiles, but I see the concern in his eyes.

"Sure," I reply. He adds another five pounds to my weights and I feel the resistance as I finish ten more reps.

Scarlet removes her bands and watches me for a few moments. She crosses the room and taking Jacob's arm, pulls him toward the door of the gym.

"Wait, what's going on?" he asks.

"Come on, let's give them some privacy," Scarlet says softly, although I hear her plainly. They close the door behind them. I lower the weights and stand.

"I know you're worried about Christian. I am too. Vivica assures me that once we have a demand from Castillo, we'll know how to respond," Dante says.

"What does that mean? You know she won't trade Christian for me or for the artifacts."

Dante hesitates and then says, "No. Probably not."

"Well, that's what Castillo's going to want. You and I both know it. We can't wait, Dante. We have to recue Christian before Castillo decides he's not worth anything to him and kills him. You know he'll do it."

Dante looks at me for a long moment. He drops his eyes and nods. He knows I'm right.

"I know it's not the way you do things, that you always follow Vivica's lead, but I have a plan that I think will work. I need you to trust me."

"I do trust you, Grace. I just don't want to see you hurt," Dante says, brushing a loose strand of hair behind my ear. "I just got you back. I don't want to lose you again."

He cups my face in with his hand and I stare deep into his blue eyes.

"I'll help you with your plan, but ultimately your safety will be my first concern, okay?" he says softly.

I nod into his palm and he kisses my forehead, and then my cheek. His mouth hovers over mine for a moment before his lips tenderly touch mine. The kiss deepens as I step closer and his arms tighten around me. His hands slide down my back and suddenly our mouths and tongues are hungrily devouring each other.

"Oh man, sorry, uh, I'll just come back later."

Dante and I jump apart to see Alejandro backing towards the door, his face red. I pull away and smile. Alejandro is just the person I want to talk to.

"No, come in," I say quickly. "I wanted to talk to you, anyway."

Alejandro crosses to the shelves filled with weapons and picks up a knife, lovingly caressing the blade, his cheeks pink.

"What I can do for you?" he asks, but I think he already knows. Christian and Alejandro go way back. I'm sure he's as anxious as I am to find his friend.

"We're going to get Christian," I say firmly, sliding my

hand in Dante's. "It will be a small team. We're flying under the radar, if you know what I mean."

Alejandro nods, turns and throws the dagger at the target hung across the room. It hits the bullseye dead center with a dull twang. He nods, satisfied.

"I'm in, Grace. Just tell me when and I'll be there. I'd like to include Elena on this mission, if that's alright with you. She's an expert in knives and the crossbow."

"Okay," I nod, a team beginning to form. A slow smile spreads across my face. We're going to do this.

FOURTEEN

CHRISTIAN

I must have dozed for a few minutes because I jolt awake as someone stomps down the stairs. It's the Vagary girl from earlier. She drops a bottle of water by my head and studies me. I take in her black boots and long legs encased in dark jeans. Her black t-shirt hugs her curves in all the right places. My eyes travel to her face and she folds her arms across her chest and glares at me.

"I don't get it. Why would you help the Kairos? You know they're only using you," she says, although a pink blush creeps across her cheeks at my scrutiny. Okay, I'll admit she's pretty hot for a Vagary, even with the black eye, but I try not to let that distract me.

"Uh, what did you say?" I mumble. I don't think I heard her

right. Did she say the Kairos were the evil ones? She touches her swollen lip briefly and frowns at me.

"Don't blame me. That would be Avery. She's a black belt in Karate. I'd stay away from her from now on, if I were you," I say. I can't help teasing her. She's even prettier when she's mad.

"Oh, you... stupid Kairos," she stammers, and turning around heads back to the stairs.

"Wait. I'm sorry. Don't leave mad," I say.

What am I doing? Am I really flirting with this Vagary girl, while I'm being held prisoner by Castillo? I must be out of my mind, but maybe I can soften her up and get some information that will help me get out of here.

She turns around and eyes me suspiciously.

"What?" she asks, arms folded across her chest.

"I'm a little hungry. Do you think you could bring me something to eat?" I say. I try to put on a puppy dog look of pleading.

She frowns, so I add, "Just anything. A piece of bread, a granola bar, whatever."

Her face softens a little bit and I press my advantage. "Also, it's pretty cold down here, could I get a blanket?" Her face hardens again.

"Too much?" I ask, innocently. Her cheeks turn pink again.

"Oh, you...you," She whirls around and stomps back up the stairs. I sigh, and lay back on the hard concrete. It was worth a try. It must be late evening by now, although I don't have a watch so there's no way to tell. There are no windows down here and the little bit of light is from a dim bulb in the corner of the room. I grab the water bottle and drink half before deciding I better save the rest. I wasn't kidding about being hungry. I only had a cup of coffee before the battle this morning and my stomach growls noisily.

The door opens quietly at the top of the stairs and the Vagary girl slips inside and slowly tip-toes down the stairs like she doesn't want anyone to hear. She crossed to me and lays a banana and a granola bar down beside me. She steps back quickly as if she's afraid I might grab her.

The food looks like ambrosia to me. I sit up slowly, my shoulder protesting the movement.

"Do you have a name?" I ask, peeling the banana, before taking a huge bite. I don't think I've ever tasted anything so good in my entire life.

She hesitates, before finally saying, "Hannah."

"Nice to meet you, Hannah. I'm Christian," I say. "Thanks for the food."

Hannah nods, shifting nervously from one foot to the other, then looks behind her up the stairs. "I better go. Just do what Castillo wants, okay. Then you won't get hurt."

"It's not quite that black and white," I say. "You don't know the whole story, or you wouldn't ask that of me."

"I know the Kairos have kidnapped Castillo's Great Niece. They have brainwashed her and won't let her go," Hannah says, defensively. I shake my head. It's not that simple.

"Do you know where I came from? Or when?" I ask. Hannah shakes her head.

"I was born in Kansas City, Missouri, August 13th, 2048."

Her mouth falls open and she takes a step back.

"Really?" she asks.

I nod. "Yup, I know about the Vagaries because I lived through it. You have no…" I break off as footsteps clomp down the wooden stairs. Norm scowls at Hannah.

"What are you doing down here?" he ask. His eyes narrow when he sees the food. Hannah shrugs, brushes past him and climbs the stairs quickly. Norm scowls at me, looking like he's thinking about punching me again, but follows Hannah up the stairs, closing the door firmly behind him.

I swallow back my disappointment. It shouldn't bother me what this Vagary girl thinks, but somehow it does. She's been fed a bunch of lies. Not my problem, I remind myself and try to put Hannah out of my mind. I need to find a way out of here. I swallow the granola bar in two bites as I look around the basement. There's not much down here, except concrete and that old rusty boiler. It's probably been out of use for fifty years. Luckily, I'm not tied up or restrained, probably because of my injury. There's no way out of here, anyway.

I stand to test my strength. My head spins a bit, but slowly clears. The portal almost completely healed my knife wound when I travelled to New York City. If I could somehow get out of here and find another portal, I could get back to Kairos house and heal myself at the same time.

Walking the perimeter of the small room, I search the walls for any kind of crack or weakness. It's solid, made out of cinder blocks filled with concrete. I'm not getting out that way. When I reach the boiler, I examine it carefully. I wonder if I could make a weapon out of part of it. Upon closer inspection, I realize the pipes are so old they are rusted tight. I sigh. Come on, I need a break.

I'm just about to give up when I notice a small piece of wood about two feet square, partially hidden behind the boiler. Painted grey, it blends in with the wall, and in the dim light is almost invisible. What could be behind that? Maybe nothing, but if it's a crawl space, I could be in luck. I get on my hands and knees and squeeze into the space behind the boiler. The wood is nailed in place but I can tell it's been there a while and one of the nails is loose, hanging half out of the board. I wish I had a hammer. I'd have it removed in no time. I'll just have to use my hands.

I work at the loose nail and I remove it easily. The others will take more effort, but I'm determined. It might be a dead end, but right now it's my only hope of escape.

It takes me a good fifteen minutes to remove another nail, but once I do that, I'm able to get my fingers underneath the board and pry the wood away from the wall. I'm so relieved to see a crawl space, I want to shout, or high-five someone. I'll celebrate after I'm out of here, though. I peer into the dark hole wishing I had a flashlight.

I pull my body into the narrow space and turn around to replace the wood. I can't really secure it, so I lean it against the wall as best I can and hope no one sees it. Of course, as soon as they realize I've escaped, it won't take them long to find the crawl space.

It's dark under the house, and the space is only two feet high. I push away my natural claustrophobia. I won't even think about the spiders that live under here. I shudder. I consider myself a tough guy and their isn't much that scares me. Except spiders. I *hate* the little crawling things.

I pray my eyes will adjust to the darkness enough to see a way out. I've only crawled forward about ten feet when I hear voices and a shout. Damn it. They've discovered I'm gone. I crawl faster, glancing around frantically for a sliver of light to guide me to an opening. I realize that it's dark outside now, and curse my luck. I keep moving, though. Eventually, I have to find the way out of here. I hope.

FIFTEEN

GRACE

We gather in Dante's room at midnight. I watch as Alejandro and Elena wander the space admiring all of the paintings displayed about the room. Dante's painting of me in Paris hangs on the wall by the fireplace. I touch the frame gently, gazing at the soft dreamy quality of the work. So much has happened since I first saw this painting.

Dante and I decided to keep the team small. The less people who know what we're up to, the better. I glance in the mirror above the dresser and take in my boots, black jeans, and leather jacket. With my hair pulled back into a pony tail and the Ambitus strapped to my belt, I look ready for a fight.

Dante enters and closes the door quietly behind him.

"It's all clear. We're good to go," he says.

"Great, but where do we start looking?" I ask.

"A note was dropped off from Castillo an hour ago," Dante says.

"What? Why didn't you tell me right away? What did it say?" I ask, impatiently.

"I wanted to discuss it with everyone and decide our plan of action."

"Let's hear it," Alejandro says, as Elena steps closer to listen.

"He's demanding an exchange. But it wasn't what we thought it would be. It isn't you he wants, Grace. It's the Ambitus," Dante says.

"So much for the claim that he wanted to get to know me better. Well, he can't have the Ambitus *or* Christian," I say flatly, my hand automatically going to the dagger at my waist.

"I managed to catch up with the messenger. I talked to him and I have a piece of information we can use. He wasn't a Vagary and didn't have a definitive address of origin, but he brought the note from New Jersey. We'll begin our search at the Vagaries' residence there."

"I'm ready," I say. "but how will we get to New Jersey?" I ask. I didn't think about that.

"Kairos house portal," Dante says. "It's the fastest way and I've already located a secure portal a few miles from the Vagaries' residence."

Elena nods, and slips on a long dark blue jacket. She fastens the crossbow and quiver across her back. Dante's sword is hidden under his long trench coat. I have no idea the number of knives Alejandro has hidden on his body, but I'm sure it's at least ten. Having these fierce Kairos by my side gives me hope that we'll be successful and rescue Christian.

We slip out of Dante's room and have just begun to tip-toe down the stairs when Scarlet opens her door and slips into the hall, tightening the belt to her robe around her slim waist.

"I knew you were up to something," Scarlet says, glancing at us where we stand frozen on the stairs. She crosses to me.

"Where are you going?"

"I have to get Christian. I can't leave him with Castillo," I say, urgently. "You understand, don't you?"

"I suppose," Scarlet says, "Just be careful, okay?" I nod, and she rubs my arm, concern on her pretty face.

Scarlet shoots Dante a meaningful *you should know better* look , then returns to her room, shutting the door quietly behind her. I breathe a sigh of relief.

We continue down the stairs to the grand foyer. I try to walk softly, but my boots echo on the polished marble floor. Dante punches in the combination on the lock and swings open the door to the portal. Alejandro and Elena follow us inside. Weapons line the shelves, ready for use at a moment's notice.

We face each other and join hands to ensure we end up in the same place.

"I'll get us there," Dante whispers, "Try to relax and go with the portal." I nod, noticing the stone on the Ambitus at my waist glows green. Dante tightens his hold on my hand. Our eyes lock as the portal activates and we're spinning through time once more.

It seems like mere moments before we arrive at the New Jersey portal. The spinning slows and I look around me. We're outside, surrounded by beautiful tree branches. The stars sparkle overhead. We step away from the portal and I gasp at the Manhattan skyline, and the Statue of Liberty lit up in the distance, sweeping views of the Hudson River between us.

"It's beautiful." I breathe, admiring the view.

"This is Liberty State Park. I'll bring you back when we have time to enjoy it," Dante whispers, "Right now we have a Kairos to rescue."

"Right," I say. I have a mission to complete. We follow Dante through the park, staying close to the trees and out of the lamps that illuminate the area. As we near the exit, Dante motions for us to gather around him.

"Once we leave the park, it's about a mile to the Vagary residence," he says, "We can't just waltz in there. We have to be smart and figure out where they are holding him and the best way to extricate him."

I grip the Ambitus and close my eyes. Come on, I think, show me Christian. Slowly a picture forms in my mind. I can't see him very clearly as he's in a dark place. He's moving strangely. Is he seriously hurt, I wonder? No, no, I think he's… crawling. That's strange. I try to see more details, but it's too dark. At least I know he's alive.

"I see him. He's crawling along the ground, but I can't tell where he is. It's too dark. I don't know if he's in the Vagary's house or somewhere else," I say. I close my eyes again and ask the Ambitus to guide me to Christian.

Green light shoots out in front of me. Okay, then. We'll go that way.

Dante takes my free hand and we walk along the street. I hear cars and other street noises in the distance, but it's fairly quiet where we are. The cool night air seeps through my jacket and I shiver. Dante pulls me close to his side and we pick up the pace.

"I never thought I'd be in New Jersey," Alejandro says, quietly. Of course he hasn't. Until a few days ago he'd never been out of Missouri.

"New Yorkers like to give it a hard time, but it's not bad, really," I whisper as we turn the corner onto Johnston Avenue.

"The house is a few blocks down on the left," Dante says. My heart rate picks up. I'm not looking forward to the inevitable confrontation with Castillo, but it can't be helped. We walk past several stately homes, complete with iron gates and security cameras. I hadn't thought about that. *Of course* they will have security surrounding the house. How will we even get near it, let alone find Christian?

"We have a problem," I say, my steps slowing. "If the Vagaries house is gated, how will we get inside? I mean, it's not like we can ring the doorbell and pretend to be selling cookies or something."

Elena giggles. "You know, I was behind a tree with my crossbow during the battle this morning. I don't think any of the Vagaries saw me. I could make contact; maybe even get inside the gate."

"I don't like it. What if they realize you're a Kairos. Then we'll have to rescue you along with Christian," Alejandro says.

"Unless they test me in a portal, I don't think they'll know," Elena replies.

"I doubt they'll let a stranger in anyway. There's got to be a better way," Dante says as we resume walking. "Let's pass by on the other side of the street and take a look."

We cross the street and stay in the shadows.

"It's that one on the corner." Dante points to a beautiful red brick tutor home, all light stucco and dark beams. Of course it's surrounded by a large red brick wall with a wrought iron gate at the driveway entrance. There are several lights on inside the house. The Ambitus vibrates in my hand, the light shooting towards the gate.

"He's in there, alright," I say, nodding to the dagger.

"Hmm," Alejandro says. "This won't be easy."

"We'll have to climb over the wall and if Christian is injured it might be impossible to get him out that way," Dante adds.

"I have an idea," Elena says, "We could create a diversion. One that has them opening the gates."

"Okay, go on," Dante says.

"Well, um, there's something I haven't told you about myself. I sort of have a thing for explosives. It's kind of my passion," She says almost sheepishly.

"Are you telling us you have explosives with you.. now?" Dante asks, his eyes widening in surprise.

Elena opens her jacket and displays a clear tube filled with a grey clay substance. Oh my gosh, I think she has explosives strapped to her shoulder. She unzips a pocket inside her jacket and pulls out a plastic bag filled with wires and things. I also see several firecrackers and a match book. I blink, then shake my head. The girl is prepared.

"This is my emergency kit. I bring it on all my assignments. Just a little C-4, and a detonator, among other things," she says, as if it's no big deal.

Just a little C-4, I think…oh my heck. This is too perfect. We might just have a chance. Alejandro's eyes bug out of his head. He whistles softly.

"Okay. I'm seriously impressed," he says. If he wasn't in love with Elena before, he is now.

"How does it work?" I ask.

"Well, C-4 is a very stable plastic explosive and can't be detonated by a gunshot or by dropping it onto a hard surface, or anything like that. It doesn't explode when set on fire either, so it's safe for me to carry. An explosion occurs when a detonator inserted into it is fired...by me." Elena shows us the detonator in her hand.

"What's your plan, then," Dante asks.

"It's simple. We set the explosive into the wall by the gate, then climb over the wall, away from the entrance and the cameras. Once inside, we detonate the C-4. When the Vagaries come outside to investigate, we search the house for Christian."

"It could work," Dante says, "as long as everything goes according to plan."

"I think we should try it. I certainly don't have a better idea," I say. I check with the Ambitus again. "Christian is still in that dark space."

"Okay. We'll try it," Dante says.

Alejandro rubs his hands together. "Let's go Amigos."

We check one more time to make sure no one is around and run quickly across the street and along the wall to the corner.

"I'll cover Elena while she sets the explosive," Alejandro says. They creep down the sidewalk, stopping about five feet from the gate. It only takes about thirty seconds before they're back.

"Alright." She holds the detonator in her hand and says, "Ready whenever you are."

"Good. Let's go," Dante replies. We walk along the wall until we are a few feet past the house. Alejandro gives Elena a boost and she quickly scales the block wall. He follows. Dante assists me over next, then with a running leap he grabs the top of the wall and flings his legs over, landing softly on his feet. I can see why the Kairos train so much.

We run across the lawn and crouch down next to the house. My heart beats so loudly it fills my ears. I swallow as Dante nods, and Elena presses the detonator. One second later, the C-4 explodes, sending bricks and mortar flying in all directions. Smoke and dust fills the air. I hear voices and then shouts as the Vagaries run outside. Now is our chance.

We slip around the back. I search for a window to the basement, but don't see anything except a small grate. I wonder if it leads to a crawl space under the house. Maybe there is no basement. I keep looking. If we can't find a basement window we may have to enter the house through the main floor and I really don't want to do that. We hear voices and sprint around to the back. We don't want to be caught before we even have a chance to look. I grip the Ambitus and the green light points into the house. Christian is in there. I pray we find him quickly before Castillo is onto us.

SIXTEEN

CHRISTIAN

Light flashes, briefly illuminating the small space, followed by a loud explosion. I immediately see an opening, and crawl towards it, but my shoulder is aching again and its slow going. I don't know what caused the explosion, but I allow myself a glimmer of hope that it's the Kairos. Maybe I'll make it out alive after all.

I reach the metal grate and grimace when I see the spiders clinging to it. I push against the metal anyway, sending my new arachnid friends scurrying away. It falls forward easily. I might just have something go my way, for once. The opening isn't big, and I hope I don't end up stuck, but I have to try. I barely wiggle through, and stand up, grateful to be out of the small space, just as the Vagaries round the corner of the house.

Damn, can't I catch a break?

"Hey! Stop," the hulk says, running toward me. Adrenalin pumps through me and I turn to face him. At least I can defend myself now. I don't have a weapon, but I have my fists. I push past the pain in my shoulder as he reaches me. I attack with a right hook to the jaw, followed by a kick to his groin. Norm looks surprised before grabbing his crotch, moaning. I follow with a punch to his gut.

"Not very pleasant is it, Norm," I say, and kick his knees out from under him. He falls on the ground clutching his stomach.

"Well, I see you enjoy the fight," a voice behind me says. I turn to see Castillo and several Vagaries. Hannah is with them, her hands on her hips, but I notice a small pang of sympathy cross her face.

"Hold him." Two of the Vagaries grab me, twisting my arms behind my back. I gasp as pain shoots through my shoulder.

Castillo walks slowly around me and shakes his head. "What a nuisance you've become. I think you need to be taught a lesson. You're a competent fighter, but how would you fair in a real test of skill?"

Hannah gasps behind him, and he turns and looks at her. She covers her mouth with her hand, eyes huge in her pale face. His eyes narrow.

"You feel sorry for this Kairos, do you, my dear? Maybe you helped him escape? Maybe you've been working with the

Kairos all along."

"No," Hannah says, shaking her head, but I can see Castillo doesn't believe her. I think Hannah is about to discover his true colors.

"I know just the place for both of you." He motions to the Vagaries and they grab Hannah tightly by her arms. She protests, but Castillo turns around and slaps her across the face. She stumbles back, shocked.

We're marched to the front of the house and up the stone stairs to the door. Castillo enters and we're shoved inside. The entry is massive with stone archways and columns. Gold leaf is everywhere and the ceiling is painted to resemble something out of the Sistine chapel, all angels and devils locked in battle. We're dragged through a door to the right into a formal room, complete with gold velvet couches and a black grand piano.

"You are the only Kairos in history of our great conflict to enter my personal portal. It's quite a privilege really. You see, you are going far, far away, so far that no one will ever find you." Castillo smiles, removing his coat. He opens a closet and pulls out a length of gold silk cloth, fastening it about him in a toga style. The ends drapes over his shoulders and down his back. He looks like frickin' Julius Caesar or something. Unease creeps down my spine.

"Have you ever wondered who were the greatest warriors of all time? Some might argue that it was the Berserker, the elite Viking warriors, or possibly the Japanese Samurai. But

I would disagree. I believe the greatest warriors on earth were the Roman Gladiators. Soon, you will have the great honor of experiencing this for yourself."

Two Vagary guards, both beefy looking guys in their twenties, arm themselves also, but not with swords. They each holster pistols complete with extra magazines in their jackets. They certainly are going prepared.

Castillo flings open double doors to a portal unlike anything I've ever seen before. The walls are painted blood red with plush red carpet covering the floor. Gold damask fabric is gathered to the center of the ceiling and a crystal chandelier hangs downs the middle of the room, almost touching the carpet. It's gorgeous and hideous at the same time.

We're shoved inside along with Castillo and the two Vagaries holding us. I glance at Hannah and see she's been crying, a red hand mark on her pale cheek. I feel bad that I somehow got her mixed up in this.

The doors are pulled shut and we are instantly spinning through time. I try to think of Kairos house and wonder if I could somehow transport us all there, but I can tell it's not working. My stomach lurches as the colorful lights circle around us. The red portal falls away and we fly through time.

SEVENTEEN

GRACE

The back door opens and we dive behind a large hedge. Castillo and several Vagaries pass by and turn the corner to the side of the house.

"Come on," I whisper. "We need to see what they're doing."

"Should Alejandro and I search the house?" Elena asks. Dante nods.

"Be careful. If you don't find Christian, or if it's too dangerous, meet back at the park," he says. They nod, and take off toward the house.

Dante and I peer around the corner in time to see two Vagaries restraining Christian. He's surrounded. I glance at Dante but he holds me back, hesitant to take them on. I'm surprised when Castillo turns to the Vagary girl, slapping her across the face. The other Vagaries grab the girl too and march them both to the front house.

I shake my head. I'll never understand the Vagaries.

As soon as they are out of sight, we follow. I notice the grate I'd seen earlier is now on the ground and it suddenly makes sense. Christian *was* in the crawl space. If only I'd realized sooner. I take the Ambitus in both hands, close my eyes, and ask to see Christian.

He's in one of the rooms inside the house, and Castillo is dressed in some kind of strange red robe. It looks like a toga type outfit. Dante grabs my arm and my eyes fly open. Alejandro and Elena are back. Alejandro shakes his head.

"We need to get out of here," he whispers. "More Vagaries are on their way from other houses in New York."

I nod, heartsick at being so close and unable to rescue Christian. We climb the wall once more and head back to the portal. I glance at the hole in the block wall around the Vagaries house. At least we did some damage tonight. I won't give up, though. I know Christian is alive. That's something.

When we travel back to Kairos house, I half expect to be met by Vivica demanding to know where we've been, but the house is quiet. I tip-toe up the stairs, and slip into Scarlet's room. She's asleep, but wakes even though I try to be quiet.

"You're back. Any luck?" she asks.

"No. We saw Christian, so I know he's still alive, but there were too many Vagaries around. We weren't able to get close to him."

"I'm sorry. Try to get some sleep, Grace. We'll talk to Vivica in the morning and see what can be done," Scarlet says.

I wash my face and brush my teeth as a slow anger begins to burn inside of me. Doesn't Christian deserve a little worry? A plan to rescue him? Shouldn't we be doing more than just 'we'll talk about it in the morning.'

I place the Ambitus on the table beside my bed and slip beneath the covers. I sigh, flinging my arm over my eyes. The events of the evening replay over and over in my mind. Life was a lot simpler when I was just a normal high school teenager worried about the next A.P. Calculus test.

EIGHTEEN

CHRISTIAN

The spinning stops and we land with a thud onto hard ground. I glance around the dim space. We are in some kind of a stable or shed. The air is warm, like a summer's evening, but it also stinks. The smell of animal feces and rotten food hangs heavy in the air. A small torch illuminates the area, causing black soot to waft through the air, adding to the stench.

The Vagary guards who accompanied us here, assist Castillo to his feet, while he adjusts his robe. The door opens and a little man appears. I mean, he's really a *little* man, as he's only three feet tall and has dwarfism. He's dressed in a simple brown tunic, with a leather belt around his waist and sandals on his feet. He has messy unkempt hair and a hooked nose. A prominent scar runs down the right side of his face.

"Ah, Lino, there you are. Please tell the Emperor I have arrived and require an audience immediately," Castillo says. He holds out his hand with the Vagary ruby ring. Lino rushes forward, kisses the ring, and scurries away.

I hear the words Castillo says, but although I realize he's speaking in an ancient language, possibly Latin, my mind processed it into English. I understood everything.

"Where are we?" I ask Castillo.

"You'll find out soon enough, boy. Let's just say you're not in Kansas City anymore." He laughs softly, and rubs his hands together. He's really enjoying this, sadistic bastard.

Hannah stands beside me glancing around with wide, frightened eyes. I don't blame her. Wherever we are, I have a sinking feeling it's not going to be a pleasant visit.

The Vagary guards seem unafraid, but I also notice their hands rest on their guns, and they look a little green around the edges. I rotate my shoulder experimentally, and am relieved to feel no pain. The portal healed my wound, thank God, because I have the feeling I'm going to need the use of my shoulder.

Lino reappears in the doorway.

"Veni," he says, which means, *come.* He motions for us to follow him.

Lino is flanked by four soldiers dressed in Roman attire, complete with iron breast plates and helmets. Wicked looking swords swing from the belt at their waists. They eye us suspiciously. Our clothing is totally wrong for this era. This is not good.

We enter a passageway with wood planked ceilings that hang low overhead. The path we walk on is paved with dark red bricks. The walls are stone and wood. We pass several more stalls and I see a huge black horse in one of them eating hay from a trough. I hear the feral roar of a lion in the distance, and my heart stops. I'm afraid I know exactly where we are. I'd read about this place in a history book years ago. If I'm right, we are in the Gladiators quarters, underneath the Roman Colosseum. We turn into a tunnel that slopes down as we walk and takes us underground.

Hannah stays close to my side. She bites her lip as she looks around nervously. I can feel her body shaking with fear. I don't blame her. To be honest, I'm terrified also.

We walk for about five minutes, an occasional torch lighting the tunnel in front of us. Rat droppings litter the ground and the scurry of tiny rodent feet, just adds to the ambiance. I shake my head. I need to get my wits about me. I have the feeling I'm about to meet a Roman Emperor. Most of them were vicious, egotistical tyrants. If this one developed a relationship with Castillo, he might be even worse. Yup, this will probably end badly. The tunnel begins to slope upward and we approach a massive wooden door. Another soldier stands guard, but steps aside as we near.

Lino pushes the heavy wooden door open. We enter what I assume is the Emperors palace. These people sure like marble. It's everywhere...on columns, and arches, and polished to a high shine under our feet. Fresco paintings of toga clad women decorate the walls and ceiling. Yeah, not really my thing. I'm sure some historian dude would love to see this, but I think it's awful. At least it smells a little better in the Palace. Incense and floral arrangements replace the stink of animal crap. It's an improvement.

A bald, heavy set man in a brown and tan toga rushes toward us. Jewels sparkle on every finger of his outstretched hands. He takes Castillo's hand in his, kissing the ruby ring.

"Aemilius, you're looking well," Castillo says in Latin with a regal nod of his head, as if he is the Emperor.

"Yes, by the will of the Gods," Aemilius says, adjusting the cloth over his wide girth.

"We haven't heard from you in months. Emperor Commodus was rather upset. But you're here now, so no matter," Aemilius says with a sigh.

He eyes Hannah and I, then glances at the Vagary guards. He turns to Castillo. "All is well in the future time?" Aemilius asks.

"We are dealing with a small matter, but it will soon be resolved. I require some assistance with these two." Castillo gestures to Hannah and I.

"Yes. Yes. How may we serve you?"

"First they need proper clothing. These two are trained

fighters so they need to be under guard at all times." Aemilius nods as he gazes at me, but frowns as he takes in Hannah's slim form.

"Even the girl?" he asks.

"I trained her myself. She can be quite deadly if given the opportunity. Don't give her the chance." Aemilius looks Hannah over, a glint in his eye that I don't like.

A tall door opens and the person who enters must be Emperor Commodus. His toga is a rich ruby red, fastened at the shoulder with gold leaves and pearls as big as marbles. He's about six feet tall with dark hair, cropped short. He has a high forehead and prominent chin. As he nears, I see his eyes are small and dark brown. If it wasn't for the cruel twist to his thin lips, he might have been handsome. My muscles tense instinctively. This guy is bad news. I feel it in my bones. I shift uncomfortably. Damn, I would give anything for a weapon right now.

"Xavier, welcome. It's been a long time. I wondered if you had forgotten about your friends here in Rome," the Emperor says, almost pouting.

"Of course not." Castillo nods, smiling. He watches Commodus intently, as do the Vagary guards, and I wonder if Castillo trusts the Emperor either.

"Did you bring it?" Commodus says, stepping closer to Castillo. Castillo nods and motions to one of the Vagary guards, who pulls a brown pill bottle from the inside of his jacket. He hands it to Castillo.

"You're sure it's safe. How do I know it's not poison?" the Emperor asks.

"Here, I'll show you." Castillo opens the bottle and hands it to Commodus. "Pick one and I'll swallow it." The Emperor chooses one and after Castillo swallows the pill, with no harmful effect, Commodus smiles brightly.

"This will heal your ailment, but take care from now on. I won't always be available to offer assistance," Castillo says, so quietly I almost don't hear. "As a show of gratitude, what may I do for you?" the Emperor asks.

"These two prisoners are trained Kairos fighters. I know how much you enjoy sport, so naturally I thought of bringing them to you. Rome has such excellent warriors to challenge their skills."

"Hmm," Emperor Commodus says, slowly walking around us. "The male is well formed. I'm sure we have several Gladiators to match him, but the girl?" He laughs, shaking his head.

"Don't be fooled. She's trained and can hold her own," Castillo says.

Commodus shrugs. "As you wish. We'll take them to the Gladiators quarters and dress them appropriately. We have the games scheduled in a few days, but it's always nice to have a small exhibition before... a warm up to the main event."

"Do you understand what they're saying?" I whisper to Hannah. She shakes her head, eyes wide. She's recovered a

107

bit of her strength and isn't shaking anymore. She would be terrified if she knew what Castillo was planning, though.

"Do *you*?" she asks, quietly.

"Yeah. They are going to make us change our clothing," I warn her. Her eyes go even wider, if possible, and she begins to shake again. My protective instincts kick into gear and I wonder if there is a way to keep her with me or if we'll be separated. I glance at the Roman guards…probably not.

Commodus waves a hand and the guards move toward us.

"Take them to the Gladiator's quarters. Prepare them to fight in the morning." He waves a hand in our direction. It's then that I notice the Vagary ruby ring on Commodus's little finger. Damn. If Commodus is a Vagary we are all in big trouble.

NINETEEN

GRACE

I pick at the cinnamon roll Juanita insisted I eat. I give up and push it away. I'm too worried. What did Castillo do with Christian? I tried to find him with the Ambitus as soon as I woke up this morning, but all I could see was a room with a lit torch on the wall. He could be anywhere.

"Tell me again what you saw," Dante prompts.

"Well, it was just a room. I didn't see Christian. I don't know. I could barely see anything."

"But you *could* see the room. What was in it?" he asks, taking my hand and rubbing the back gently with his thumb.

"Well, it had a dirt floor," I say, trying to remember every detail. "There was a wooden bench against a stone wall and a torch hanging above it."

"Okay. That's a start. Anything else?"

I close my eyes and picture the room again. As it comes into focus, I notice a few more things. A sword and helmet lay on the floor next to the bench.

"Oh my gosh, I remember something else." I unzip my backpack and pull out a notebook and pencil. "I'm not an artist, like you, but I'll try to draw what I saw."

I sketch the sword with its wooden handle and wide tip. The helmet, which came down across the cheek bones, had a plume of feathers curving over the top.

"Okay. Yeah, I think I know where you're going with this. May I?" he asks, and I hand him the pencil.

"Of course. I told you I'm not an artist."

He reworks my simple sketch and within a few minutes, I'm looking at a Roman sword and helmet. I know it and so does Dante. It's so obvious. He looks at me and smiles, but his eyes are grim.

"Do you think we can find him?" I ask.

"Maybe. I don't know." He shakes his head and glances at the sketch once more. "We'd need more information. Places, and dates. The Romans ruled for over a thousand years and over a large area that spanned almost all of Europe."

I slump back in my chair. "We'll just have to get more information."

Dante stands, and places my plate on top of his. He sets them in the kitchen sink.

"I'll get the Ambitus and try again," I say.

"Sure, whatever you want to do." He picks up the sketch. "I'll talk to Vivica and see what she suggests."

"Thank you," I say, looking up into his gorgeous blue eyes. He kisses my head and leaves the kitchen.

Pushing down my frustration, I hope we have a plan of action soon. I slip the notebook and pencil into my backpack. It seems empty without the Challis and Flag weighing it down. I slip it over one shoulder and head to my room. I'm half way up the stairs when I stop in my tracks. Of course. What was I thinking? I need *all* of the artifacts to discover exactly where Christian is. I race up the stairs and into the bedroom. Scarlet sits on the settee, lacing up her running shoes.

"What is it? What's happened?" she asks, seeing my face.

"I need to have all the ancient artifacts together to find Christian," I say in a rush. My heart pounds with excitement. I know I'm right.

"Have you talked to Vivica about this?"

"Not yet. But why would she stop me? I'm the one that found the artifacts and brought them here. I know how to use them."

Scarlet shrugs. "I just know how cautious Vivica can be sometimes."

I cross to my bedside table and retrieve the Ambitus. Walking back to the settee, I sit next to Scarlet and place the Ambitus in her hand.

"Um, what are you doing?" she asks.

"What happens when you hold this dagger?"

"Well, nothing," she says. She shrugs and hands it back to me. I return it to my backpack.

"That's my point. When *I* hold the dagger, I see.. things. It directs me to where I need to go at that time. It's the same with the other artifacts. When I use them alongside this little dagger, something magical happens. I don't know how, or why, only that it does. There has to be a reason for it, and I think it's for events like this. If I can't use them to help my own Kindred, then why have them at all."

"You're preaching to the choir, Grace. I believe you. You need to talk to Vivica."

"I will," I say, jumping up. "I'll talk to her right now."

Scarlet nods, and I rush out of the room once more. I stop at the top of the stairs. Should I go to Vivica's private rooms or see if she's in the library? It's only eight o'clock. Maybe she's not awake yet. I hesitate, unsure what to do, when I hear Dante's muffled voice coming from down the hall. I turn and walk along the landing that overlooks the grand entry to the hallway on the other side. I've never been over here, as Vivica's rooms are on this side of the house. I tread lightly on the carpet until I'm in front of the door. I hear more muffled voices and lean close. I want to hear what they're saying.

"We have to do what's best for everyone, not just what Grace wants," Quinton is saying.

"It's not that simple," Dante replies.

"Let's focus on the Swiss bank account information that Ricardo and James discovered," Vivica says. "The Kairos need that money, Dante. We run a worldwide organization, and while we have the money we need at the moment, expenses keep mounting. Clara assured me that Simon hid the money in Graces name as an insurance policy on her life. Now that she's safely with us, it's time to bring the money to the Kairos."

"Until we rescue Christian, I don't think she'll be interested in handing over that money, Vivica. I know 100 million dollars is a substantial amount, but I don't think Grace will see it that way," Dante replies.

I cover my mouth and turn around in a circle. Did I just hear that right? My father, Simon Hayes, a *Vagary*, hid 100 million dollars in an account in my name. Holy Crap. I swallow hard and press my ear against the door once more. My heart pounds so loud, I place my hand on my chest.

"Simon set up the money in a trust fund for Grace. If something happens to her in this wild goose chase to rescue Christian, the money goes to charity. We can't let that happen," Quinton adds.

"Of course I don't want anything to happen to Grace, either, but we can't hide her in Kairos house forever. I'll explain to her about the money, and what it means to us, but you need to realize that it's *her* money Vivica, left to her by her father. It's up to her to decide what to do with it," Dante says, an edge of steel in his voice.

Damn right, I think. I want to rush through that door and hug Dante. Thank God he has my back. I'm grateful to have such an amazing boyfriend on my side.

He's right about one thing...rescuing Christian is my first priority. I'll worry about the money later. If something happens to me, at least the Vagaries won't get the money, either. That makes me feel a little bit better.

I hesitate, my fist hovering in front of the door, then knock softly.

After a moment, Vivica opens the door, dressed in a navy skirt and white button up sweater. She looks surprised to see me, but recovers quickly and steps aside.

"Grace, what can I do for you?" she asks, as if she hadn't just been discussing me.

I enter her living quarters, all pale carpet, grey walls and crystal chandeliers. It beautiful in an understated, elegant way. Large windows flank a Carrara marble fireplace. I notice Excalibur, leaning against the hearth and I square my shoulders. The sword reminds me why I came to talk to Vivica in the first place.

Dante stands when I enter, and crosses the room. He slips his arm around me, pulling me to his side.

"You okay?" he asks. I nod, trying to collect my thoughts. I have a lot to say to Vivica. I decide to start with the artifacts.

"I need all the artifacts to find Christian," I say without

preamble. I cross the plush carpet and pick up Excalibur. It's heavier than I remember. I don't care. I grasp it firmly. I'm not letting it out of my sight again.

Vivica's perfect eyebrows raise in a delicate arch. "They're in my safe, where they belong," she says calmly.

Ugh, I want to shake her. She's not listening to me.

"Did *you* find the artifacts, Vivica? Was it *you* who broke into the Vagary palace to find the Flag of Macleod, or did you disguise yourself as a Vagary to steal the Golden Challis from a museum? No. That was me. That was *Christian*."

Excalibur is heavy and my arm begins to shake slightly, not from its weight really, but from emotions. Dante gently takes the sword from me before I drop it.

"I don't know why the Ambitus chose me, but it did. I can't tell you why I was able to use the artifacts to open the portals, but it happened. I think I've earned the right to use them if I need them. I *am* going to find Christine, Vivica, and I *am* going to bring him back from wherever he is. You can help me or not, but don't get in my way."

Vivica stares at me for a long moment, her fingers tapping the arm of the chair. I'm sure she's surprised by my speech, as I've always been a bit intimidated by her. I raise my chin and meet her eyes.

"Well…I see you've made up your mind," Vivica says finally, crossing the room to sit beside Quinton. "I certainly won't stop you, but don't ask me to risk the lives of the other Kairos."

"Vivica, my dear," Quinton says patiently, "this won't help you gain Grace's support in other matters, if you can't bend a little on this one."

"Oh, you mean the money?" I say. "The millions that my father left me? Yeah, I know about that, too."

Vivica's face pales and she looks at Dante.

"No, Dante didn't tell me. Although, I'm sure he was going to." I glance at Dante and he nods, taking my hand.

"I heard you talking about it just now," I say. "I don't know what I'll do with all that money, but my priority right now is Christian."

"I see I'm out numbered." Vivica says stiffly, rising to her feet. She crosses to a priceless Monet on the wall and swinging the painting to the side, reveals a large metal safe. How many of these things does she have in this house, I wonder, thinking of the safe room in the library that's hidden behind a false wall.

She quickly spins the dial several times, and pulls the door open. I see the Flag inside, the Challis laying on top. I breathe a sigh of relief. I glance at Excalibur, held tightly in Dante's grip. With the Ambitus in my backpack, and now, all the other artifacts together, I just might have a chance.

Twenty

CHRISTIAN

The soldiers lead us down the tunnel towards the Colosseum. I've yet to see anything beyond the dark Gladiator's quarters, though. My thoughts whirl around my head, mostly dread, with the added knowledge that I'm about to die. I have to admit, it will be interesting to see this historical arena in its prime, but also terrifying to fight there.

Once we reach the Colosseum, the awful smell hits me again. Man it stinks down here. We're lead down the corridor to an empty stall. One of the soldiers shoves me inside.

"Wait," I say quickly, pulling Hannah close to me. She stiffens slightly, but doesn't move away.

"This is my woman. At least give me one more night with her before I die." They eye me for a moment then laugh, nudging each other suggestively.

"We don't care. Save your strength, though. You'll need it tomorrow," One of the guards says, and they dissolve into laughter again.

Another guard enters and places two brown tunics on the bench and leather sandals on the ground beside it. He pulls off his helmet and wipes the sweat off his brow. It's warm in the small room, so I'm sure it's hot underneath all that armor.

"Don't try to leave this room. You won't get far," he says, eyeing us and our odd clothing curiously. "We've had a few like you in the past; dressed strangely and talking nonsense. They didn't last very long. You look stronger than the others, though. The Roman people love a good show and will enjoy seeing how long you last in the arena. My coin will be on the Gladiator." He grins and leaves the stall, closing the wooden door behind him, blocking it with a wide plank of wood. Yeah, we're not getting out of here until they let us out. I notice he left his helmet lying on the ground.

Hannah plops down on the bench, shaking her head. A tear slips down her cheek and she wipes it away quickly.

"I don't understand why I'm here," she says, lifting stricken eyes to mine. "I didn't do anything wrong. Why would Castillo think I'm a traitor?"

"I don't pretend to understand him," I say, uncomfortably. What I really want to say is that he's an evil Vagary, and what do you expect... but since she's a Vagary, too... I keep my mouth shut.

"Thanks for looking out for me. I'm surprised you speak the language, though," she says. I shrug. No way am I going to try to explain.

"You know what's happening tomorrow?" I ask.

"I think so. Based on where we are, I figure we're going to be fed to the lions."

"Oh, no. I'm sorry if that's what you thought, Hannah. No lions, that I know of, but I'm afraid it's not much better. We're to fight the Gladiators in an exhibition match in the morning."

Her eyes widen, but she nods, almost looking relieved.

I'm boiling, it's so hot in this small space, so I shrug out of my jacket and peel off my sweaty t-shirt. Hannah stares at my bare chest, mouth open. I smile, and hold out my hand.

"Can you hand me the largest one of those." I nod at the tunics.

"Oh yeah. Okay." Her cheeks redden and she quickly hands me a tunic.

"I'm going to change into this now so…," I say, and begin to undo my belt.

"Oh," Hannah says, and jumps up, turning her back to me. I peel off my jeans and slip the tunic over my head. It's sleeveless, but hangs down past my knees. I feel like I'm wearing a dress. It will be difficult to move in this thing. I remove my belt from my jeans and cinch it around my waist.

That helps a little bit, and at least I can move my legs freely.

I hear a sniffle and see Hannah's shoulders shake. Oh hell, she's crying again. Not that I blame her, really. We're in a hell of a mess.

"Hannah, I'm sorry you got caught up in all this," I say, and move closer to her.

She turns toward me and I slip my arms around her. She cries for a few minutes her head on my chest. When she finally looks up at me, the tears have miraculously dried up and her face is set. She steps out of my arms.

"Sorry. I'm done crying now. It's time for me to prepare to fight." I nod, and she picks up the other tunic. I turn my back while she changes.

When she's done, we study each other… two modern adults from the twenty first century, dressed in tunics, preparing to fight for our lives. We look ridiculous.

Hannah smiles, a dimple appearing in her cheek. I crack up and she joins me. I laugh until my side aches and I'm forced to take a deep breath.

"You're not so bad, for a Kairos," Hannah says.

"You're not so bad, either, for a Vagary."

"We need to have a plan. I don't know exactly what tomorrow's fight will be like, but we need to prepare as much as possible," Hannah says. Of course, she's right.

"You're a Karate master. I saw you fight, remember?" I say, "Do you have any other training or skills you can use?"

"I'm pretty deadly with a dagger. I'm okay with a sword. But I prefer the martial arts, as my speed gives me an edge."

"That's good, because I don't see a dagger anywhere around here." I pat my tunic and shrug. A corner of her mouth lifts and that dimple appears again.

"Your best option is to overwhelm your opponent with Karate, and then use his weapon against him. Let him come to you. Let him think you'll be an easy kill, then surprise him when he gets within striking distance."

Hannah nods, smoothing down the drab brown tunic that hangs to her knees.

"Practice on me. I'll pretend to come at you. Show me what you can do."

I back up until I'm against the stone wall. The room we're in isn't very big, but I'll do my best. Hannah stands in the middle looking vulnerable and lost. I pray like hell, it's just an act. I raise my hand like I'm holding a sword in the air and run towards her. She doesn't move until I'm almost on her, then whips her arm out catching me in the throat, I stumble back and she attacks with a hard kick to my groin. I fall to me knees holding my crotch.

"Oh, I'm sorry, Christian." She covers her mouth and crouches down next to me.

"I thought we were just practicing right now," I gasp through clinched teeth. I struggle not to lay on the floor in the fetal position.

Hannah's shoulders shake and I realize she's laughing. I lunge and tackle her to the ground. She grins up at me and our eyes meet. Heat flares between us. I swallow hard as her eyes travel to my mouth. Damn. I want to kiss her so bad right now, but that kind of distraction is the last thing we need.

I move away and slowly get to my feet. She stands, brushing the dirt from her hands.

"That's a good start," I say, awkwardly. "Just try and stay alive tomorrow."

"I'll do my best," she says, the gravity of the situation settling upon us.

"I'm beat. Let's try to sleep for a few hours."

Hannah nods, and we lay on the hard ground. We both struggle to find a comfortable position. These are not the best accommodations. Silence fills the room for a few minutes until Hannah whispers, "How did you become a Kairos? I mean, have you always been a time-traveler?"

I hesitate, unsure how much I should tell her. I pull a rock from underneath my back and throw it across the room. It pings against the stone wall, reminding me of the situation we're in and I think, screw it. I can tell her whatever I want. Things can't get much worse.

"I knew nothing about time-travel until I was tested as a kid. When I was able to activate a portal, the Vagaries took me to one of their youth camps. It wasn't a place I'd recommend. I ran away a few years later. Clara found me living on the

streets and I joined the Kairos. I've been with them ever since."
Thinking about those years is never pleasant, so I add, "What
about you? How did you get involved with the Vagaries?"

"I've only been traveling for a year. Most of my family
knows nothing about it. My dad is a Vagary in Seattle, and
when he discovered I could travel, sent me back East to train.
It's hard to believe the Vagaries aren't good people. I mean,
my dad is the best father a girl could ever want. Okay, I'll
admit I was shocked that Xavier Castillo would do this to me,
so I have to believe you, at least about him."

Hannah is silent for a moment and then adds, "Maybe
there's good and bad in both the Kairos and the Vagaries."

I think about it and decide she's right. Nothing is totally
black and white.

"That's probably true," I say.

A dog barks somewhere in the distance, interrupting my
thoughts, bringing me back to the reality of the situation. My
stomach twists.

Staring at the wooden ceiling, I listen as Hannah's breathing
slows and she's finally asleep. I go over the different ways I
might win a battle with a Roman Gladiator, but they all end
up with me dead.

Hannah mumbles and rolls over, her head finding my
shoulder. I tense, unsure what to do. Oh, what the hell, I
think, and pull her close to my side. She snuggles her head
under my neck and the sweet smell of honeysuckle shampoo

tickles my nose. Maybe one of us will sleep tonight, but I don't think it will be me. I groan. I do not need this kind of complication, especially now.

TWENTY-ONE

GRACE

I place the artifacts in my backpack and zip it closed. First, we have to find out where Castillo took Christian, then figure out a way to free him.

"We need a portal," I say.

"You may use the one in Kairos house," Vivica says with a resigned sigh.

"Thank you," I mumble.

"Give me a few minutes to gather a team together," Dante says.

"Okay," I say, reluctantly. I don't want to endanger the other Kindred as Vivica suggested, but maybe Dante's right. We need some help.

"Let me check with Matthew and Scarlet." Dante glances at

his watch. "Meet me at the portal in thirty minutes."

He leaves the room. Vivica closes the safe, replaces the painting on the wall, then faces me.

"I hope you aren't making a huge mistake, Grace. If these ancient treasures fall into the Vagaries hands, the world will be in mortal danger."

I nod, and swallow back a retort. I remember something my Grandpa said to me, when I was learning to ride a bike, but scared to try. Even with my helmet, knee pads and elbow guards, I was afraid I'd fall and get hurt.

"Gracey, my girl," he'd said, "People are like ships tied to a dock, they might be safe for a while, but they'll never experience true freedom that way. Ships are safe inside the harbor, but is that what ships are really for?"

I stand up straighter and nod to Vivica, closing the door firmly behind me. This ship is about to sail. I'll do my best and trust in whatever direction fate takes me.

I descend the stairs and head to the kitchen. I take a deep breath and the clean smell of lemon furniture polish tickles my nose. Now that I've made some decisions, I can't wait to get going. When I enter, Juanita is stirring something on the stove and looks up questioningly.

"Good morning, Juanita. I need a few supplies for an assignment. Maybe bread, cheese and some fruit," I suggest. It's not that I worry about me really, but who knows what shape Christian might be in when we find him.

"Of course, querida. I'll make you a sack lunch right away," Juanita says, bustling about the kitchen gathering the items. She places everything in a paper bag and hands it to me, patting me on the arm.

"You be careful. Come back to Juanita. I've lost too many Kairos and my poor heart is weary."

I nod, and hug her tightly for a moment. She's such a part of the Kindred, I sometimes forget she's not a time-traveler.

"Do you know where my mom and Henry are?" I ask.

"They were in the great room a few minutes ago," Juanita says with a smile.

I nod and place the food in my backpack. It's so full now, it barely zips closed. I think about going to see my mom and Henry, but don't think I can stand to say goodbye again. I promise myself I'll be back and will see them soon.

Juanita pats my check. She crosses herself, kissing her rosary beads, and continues to stir the pot on the stove, a constant in this house full of uncertainty.

I meet Dante right at nine o'clock sharp. Scarlet and Matthew are with him, dressed for battle and armed to the teeth. I breathe a sigh of relief. We have two of the best Kairos joining us.

Dante holds Excalibur in his right hand. He looks strong and capable and extremely dear. I gaze into his piecing blue eyes, and I realize that I might be putting his life in danger, too. I glance at Scarlet and Matthew as doubt creeps through me. What am I doing? Is Vivica right? Am I endangering all of my friends?

Dante leans forward and whispers, "We can take care of ourselves, Grace. We have trained for this for years, plus, we have help with this mission. We have you, and we have these." He lifts Excalibur and the metal glints in the sunlight streaming through the widows.

"Wait," Clara says, walking briskly into the grand foyer. She's dressed in black jeans and shirt, knives strapped to her belt.

"I'm coming with you."

I study her with wide eyes. She's a strong woman, skilled in many areas, and would be an asset to any mission.

"Really, are you sure?" I ask.

"I trained Christian. He's a dear friend and like a son to me. Of course I'm coming with you."

I nod. "I'm glad you're with us," I say, meaning it. I glance around at the team. I have some amazing Kindred and friends with me.

"We'll need these," Clara says, holding up several long hooded capes in different colors. "We can't appear in ancient Rome dressed like this." She glances around at our group dressed in battle gear. I choose a dark grey one. I slip it over my shoulders, effectively hiding my modern clothing.

The last time we used all of the artifacts together, I wrapped the flag around me and Christian used his blood to activate the Challis. We also needed six knives and Excalibur to represent the seven swords of time immortal. With the Ambitus and all the knives each person brought with them, we have everything we need.

"We'll need someone to donate blood for the challis," I say, shrugging apologetically.

"How much blood are you talking about?" asks Matthew, glancing at the Challis which is the size of a large coffee mug.

I repress the urge to giggle and say, "Just a few tablespoons."

"Okay then, I'll do it," Matthew says, shrugging as if he's not afraid of a small cut. It's going to sting like the devil, but at least traveling will heal the wound quickly.

Dante unlocks the door to the portal. We enter, and he closes it firmly behind us. I unzip my bag and pull out the Flag and Challis. I undo the Ambitus from my belt. Dante slips the flag around me and Matthew and Scarlet gasp.

"What the hell?" Matthew says, shaking his head as he walks around me looking at me from all angles.

"It really works," Scarlet whispers in amazement.

I hold the Challis in my right hand and Dante hands me Excalibur, which I take in my left.

Matthew steps forward and stretches out his arm with a grimace. I can't say as I blame the guy. Dante slices Matthew's arm and a line of bright red blood wells up, dripping down his arm to his wrist. I hold the Challis underneath while his blood drips inside. It's barbaric, but necessary.

Clara wraps a clean cloth around Matthew's forearm and

ties it tightly.

"Swords out," Clara says, and I hold the Ambitus to Excalibur as the rest of the team places their sword against the metal. As soon as the last knife hits the Excalibur's blade, the portal activates.

I close my eyes and ask the Ambitus to take me to Christian wherever is he is *right now*, in this moment in time. The portal activates like a match to a flame, the Ambitus's energy igniting and surrounding us in a green swirling glow. Determination settles in my heart. This has to work. There is no other option. We hold on to each other as we fall through time.

TWENTY-TWO

CHRISTIAN

I wake with a jolt and look around. The events of the past twenty-four hours comes rushing back and I groan. My arm is pins and needles where Hannah slept on it last night, and I gently extricate myself from beneath her. A trickle of light shines through the slats of the wooden door. The night passed too quickly. I might have nodded off for a few hours, I can't be sure. My brain just wouldn't shut up. I kept trying to find a way out of this mess and coming up with nothing. I'm unsure if this exhibition fight today will be to the death, or just something to test us and prolong the torture. Either way, I'm feeling a little queasy. I can only imagine what Hannah will feel like when she wakes up.

Also, I need to pee. I look around and see a bucket in the

far corner. Oh great. I guess that's the bathroom in these luxury accommodations. I wonder how long I can hold out, but decide it's best to do it now while Hannah's still asleep. Thankfully, I manage to use the bucket without making too much noise. I'm dying of thirst, but I have a feeling if I drink any of the water in ancient Rome, I'll need to stay close to this chamber pot for the rest of the day. The last thing I need right now is to be sick. I'd give anything for the water purifier I have back in my bag at Kairos house.

Hannah stirs and sits up groggily, her hair a tangled mess of curls around her head. Her eyes widen when she sees me and the events of yesterday come rushing back.

"Oh God," she moans, flopping back onto the ground. "Tell me this is a bad dream."

"I wish it was," I say softly.

"What time is it?" she asks automatically.

I glance at my watch. Five-thirty. Still pretty early, but who knows when the guards will return. I look at my watch again; a modern timepiece that was transported with us to around 185 AD. Kind of insane when I think about it. I won't remove the watch, though, I think defiantly. Somehow, it grounds me to reality. I'm a modern man, I remind myself and I can handle this.

Hannah stands up and eyes me. After a moment she says, "You have to stay alive today. Don't leave me here alone."

"I'll do my best," I say. I wish I could promise her I'll survive today, but I can't.

She touches the tribal tattoo on my arm, tracing the lines. "This suits you." She glances up at me and then clears her throat, stepping back quickly.

"You don't happen to have a toothbrush do you?"

I pat my tunic and shrug. She smiles, and my heart gives a little leap. I tell it to shut up. I have serious things to worry about today.

"Umm, I need to go to the girls washroom. Do you think they have one of those around here?"

"Your throne awaits," I say, pointing to the pot in the corner.

Her eyes widen in horror. I move to the opposite corner and face the wall. She groans.

"This is the worst," she mutters finally, but uses the pot anyway. When she is finished she touches my shoulder and I turn around.

"When do you think they will come get us?" she asks, like I should have all the answers. It's annoying and endearing at the same time.

"I don't know. All we can do is warm up our muscles and be prepared for whatever happens."

She takes a deep calming breath and nods. She moves slowly in some kind of Tai-chi style stretching. She looks both graceful and lethal at the same time. She's really quite skilled. She'll need to be. We stretch for an hour and then sit on the ground in silence. Hannah is into some kind meditation thing, her legs crossed, her hands resting loosely on her knees. I try not to let fear creep in, but it's difficult.

The bar on the outside rattles and the door swings open. We jump to our feet.

Lino enters, followed by the two soldiers from last night. His short frame is clothed in a fine tunic of purple silk, his hair combed back. Gold bracelets adorn his wrists. He's certainly dressed up for the occasion, but it doesn't inspire confidence. One of the soldiers carries a covered basket in his arms.

"The exhibition begins soon. The Emperor has graciously allowed you to choose one weapon for today's contest. It will be given to you when you enter the arena."

Lino looks from me to Hannah, waiting for our reply. As Hannah has no idea what he's said, I choose a sword for myself and a dagger for Hannah. These weapons will do very little against an armor clad Gladiator, but it's better than nothing.

Lino rubs his hands together with excitement. He moves closer and whispers, "Are you really from the future of time?"

"Yes," I say. I might as well tell him the truth. His eyes widen, and he nods.

"I knew Xavier Castillo was from the future of time, but he never pays me any attention and I must not disrespect him, you see." He steps closer.

"Is it very different from Rome?" he continues.

"Very. We even have chariots that fly very fast through the

air," I say, dramatically. He jumps back, eyes wide.

"Ah, you're joking with Lino," he says, laughing. He shakes his head, not able to comprehend such a thing. He motions to the soldier to place the basket on the ground.

"The Emperor sends you this food with his compliments. Enjoy." Lino nods, and they exit the room, the bar on the door locking us inside once more.

Hannah opens the basket and peeks inside.

"Oh my gosh, it's food," she exclaims, pulling out a loaf of crusty bread. This is followed by some kind of dried meat, grapes, cheese and a skin filled with red wine.

We sit on the dirt floor to eat. It kind of feels like a last meal given to a condemned prisoner before the execution, but I eat it anyway. We need the strength this food will give us.

Hannah drinks thirstily from the wine flask, and I quickly take it from her.

"The last thing you need is to be intoxicated," I say, although a part of me would like to drink the whole thing and get roaring drunk. I take a small swig of the wine. It's strong stuff. The slight buzz relaxes my muscles, though. Maybe that's a good thing.

"I'm thirsty," Hannah says, around a mouth full of bread. "I'd give anything for a glass of ice water."

I nod in agreement, wishing I could give it to her. I eat a few grapes and the juice eases my thirst somewhat. I offer some to Hannah. Her eyes close and she groans as she savors the fruit, wiping a bit of juice off her chin. I look away, vowing not to be distracted. We finish eating and I slowly feel some of my strength return. I'm going to need everything I've got.

TWENTY-THREE

GRACE

As soon as the portal stops spinning, I look straight into the eyes of a goat. It bleats, and moves closer sniffing at my cloak. I shew it away, glancing around. The smell of animal dung and sweet hay tickle my nose.

We've landed in the middle of a pasture. Goats, sheep, and pigs in various pens, graze around us. Beyond that is an orchard, the trees laden with apples, pomegranates, and peaches. Rows of grapes hang heavy, ripe for the harvest. It must be late summer. A low outbuilding, which I think must be a barn, stands to my right, beyond the pasture.

Of course, ancient Rome is very different. The people are mostly farmers and merchants. This portal took us to an area surrounding the city. I decide this is a good thing, as it gives us some time to figure out where Christian is being held and formulate a plan.

Dante helps me to my feet and I take stock of our group. Everyone made it through the portal just fine, but it's hot. This could be a problem. We won't be able to wear these cloaks for long. I grasp the handle of the Ambitus and ask where we can find appropriate attire for the task at hand.

The green glow shoots to the left, down a small hill, the dirt road lined with tall, slim trees. I notice a single story house in the distance. We approach slowly, staying out of sight behind the trees. The house is built of stone with a courtyard in the middle, a covered porch on one side. This is a beautiful property and the owner must be wealthy. We creep along the side of the home and as we near an open window, I hear a woman singing. I peer inside. The woman is standing in a kitchen, kneading dough on a wooden table, her grey hair braided in a crown around her head. She wears a simple brown tunic, a red sash tied about the waist.

My love come back to me. When will the battle be over? Your child is growing and soon will be born. My love please return. I long for your embrace, she sings, her voice wobbly with age, but hauntingly beautiful. I wonder what her life has been like, what she has endured. I wish I could sit down and talk with her for hours. It would be fascinating. I'm grateful for the gift of communication the ancient artifacts has given us, though. It will be especially helpful today.

We continue walking, Dante close beside me. Clara holds up a hand, pointing to the back of the house, where long strips of cloth hang on several ropes strung between the trees. They wave gently in the warm breeze, as if to say, here I am, I've been waiting for you.

We tip-toe closer. Several tunics hang in a line. Clara hands each of us one of the tunics and slips a cream colored garment off the rope. She pulls the tunic over her modern clothing. She wraps the long strips of cloth over the tunic, Roman style. After donning my own brown tunic, I choose a lovely dark teal length of cloth, silently thanking the owner for his unknown donation to the cause. It's still warm underneath all the layers, but at least the fabric is light weight and we'll blend in with the general population. Dante wears a green toga with gold edging and Scarlet chooses a deep purple one.

"You'll need to wear this over your head," Clara says, wrapping a length of matching cloth over Scarlets head. "Your red hair will stand out like a sore thumb here."

"The curse of a ginger," Scarlet quips, securing the garment over her fiery locks.

Matthew struggles to adjust the brown tunic over his modern clothing.

"Here, let me," Scarlet says, coming to her brothers aid. I think we look pretty good until I notice my black boots peeking out from underneath the cloth. We have no time to find footwear. These boots are steel toed and great for kicking an opponent in the knee or the groin. I'm not removing them. I hide my backpack under my tunic. It sticks out one side, but isn't too noticeable unless someone is close. Excalibur is another matter. The sword is much too large to hide. I'm contemplating the problem when a voice behind us says,

"Vagary or Kairos?"

We whirl around. A man holding a sword stands behind us. Although he's not much taller than I am, he's powerfully built, his skin a dark golden brown from years in the sun. I glance at his hand for a ruby ring, but don't see one, thank God.

"Who wants to know?" Dante says, stepping in front of me, lifting up Excalibur. The man's eyes travel from the sword to Dante. He glances slowly around the group taking in his clothing that is now wrapped around us. His eyes travel to my boots.

"Welcome Kindred. I am Magnus Antonius," he says with a slight bow. "Kairos, at your service." He smiles, laugh lines fanning out from his eyes. I'd say he was about thirty years old but with the Kairos, you never know. I breathe a sigh of relief.

Dante steps forward and shakes Magnus's hand. "You're a welcome sight to be sure," he says. "Sorry about taking your clothing. We're on a mission of the utmost importance and need to borrow them."

"Of course. You may have whatever you need. Please, come inside where it is cooler. Maybe I can be of assistance."

We follow Magnus around the house and into a courtyard,

the central hub of the home. I sit on a wooden bench under the porch, the shade a welcome relief.

"Miriam, my wife, will bring you refreshments of pomegranate juice, if that's acceptable."

"Thank you, Magnus," Clara says. She introduces everyone and he nods politely.

"One of our Kindred was kidnapped by the Vagaries and brought here. This is a rescue mission," I say.

"I see," Magnus says, his eyes solemn. "I'm afraid the conditions at the moment are not favorable for the Kairos. The Vagaries are friendly with Emperor Commodus and have seized control of the city."

"Is the Emperor a Vagary, also?" I ask.

"No, but he leans on them. The Vagaries bring him gifts. I understand he enjoys that."

"Are there many Kairos in Rome?" Clara asks.

"A handful only. We do what we can to keep the Vagaries in check." He shrugs. "I am thankful you are Kairos, and have come to our aid. We could use your help."

Dante and I glance at each other. It's one thing to execute a rescue mission; quite another to defeat the Vagaries stronghold in ancient Rome.

"A Vagary named Castillo is a particular friend to the Emperor. My sources in the palace tell me he arrived last night with two prisoners."

"He *did* bring them here," I gasp. Magnus nods, and

continues.

"The message also said that an exhibition match is to be held this afternoon at the Colosseum. As a prominent land owner I am invited to these special events. I wasn't planning on attending, but now that you're here, I think I might go and bring my guests."

The woman I'd seen through the kitchen window steps into the courtyard. She's carrying a tray with goblets of juice and a platter of little oatcakes, drizzled with honey.

"This is my wife, Miriam."

"Thank you for your kind hospitality," Clara says with a smile.

Miriam nods and sets the tray on a small table.

"I'm pleased you came to us. Magnus has been pleading with the Gods for help with the Vagaries."

I glance at Dante and he raises his eyebrows. This mission has just become more complicated.

"We'll do what we can, but our priority must be our Kindred," Clara says. I'm glad she's on the same page as I am. Christian has to be our focus.

The wind picks up and blows my hair across my face. I tuck it behind my ear and take a sip from the goblet. The pomegranate juice is slightly sweet and delicious.

"Thank you, Miriam," I say, "and thank you for the clothing. This is beautiful." I run a hand over the soft fabric. She smiles, nodding her head and glances at her husband.

"Magnus is the Kairos. I'm just a simple Roman girl who fell in love with an extraordinary man. We were together for ten years before he told me about his secret life. It took me a while to accept it."

I nod. I still can't believe the turn of events that has me sitting in this courtyard in Rome, sipping juice, about to witness a match at the Colosseum.

"We have the closest portal to Rome on our land. The rest are controlled by the Vagaries. I'll have the cart and oxen prepared. It's a short distance to the city, but in this heat... better to ride than walk."

Dante reluctantly leaves Excalibur in Miriam's care. It's too large to take with us.

My heart pounds as I stand. We're going to save Christian, I think, and slip my hand under the tunic, gripping the Ambitus. We have to be victorious today... his life depends upon it.

TWENTY-FOUR

CHRISTIAN

The guards return an hour later. They snicker and suggest we use the chamber pot before we leave… thanks for that, by the way. I march along the corridor, awkwardly pulling at the tunic dress and try not to let the strange garment distract me. I have bigger things to worry about. Hannah walks beside me, chin held high. The only sign of her distress is the slight shake of her hand as she tucks a stray curl behind her ear.

I'll never understand Castillo. Why would he throw Hannah in here with me? The only thing I can figure is that he's making an example out of her, or something. He doesn't want anyone else to sympathize with the Kairos. We pass the corridor that leads to the palace. I briefly consider making a run for it, but as I'm unarmed, I doubt I'd get far. Besides, I don't want to leave Hannah. We pass the lion cages and I even see an elephant in one of the stalls. The Romans sure had strange ideas about entertainment.

We stop at a set of double doors, about ten feet wide and at least that tall. The guards push them open and the sunlight blinds me for a moment. Stone steps lead up to the arena. This is it.

"Remember, you are trained. You're strong. You can do this," I whisper to Hannah, encouragingly. In reality, I'm afraid I'm going to watch Hannah die and I won't be able to save her. I'll be fighting my own battle.

The soldiers shove us forward. We reluctantly climb the stairs and step out into the bright sunshine of the arena. The ground is covered with a mixture of course sand and dirt. The midday sun beats down hot on my shoulders.

Although large, the arena is about half the size of a football field. The surrounding structure is massive though, and can seat thousands. I take in the colorfully painted murals that line the walls. Banners overhead wave gently in the warm breeze. Cheers and applause greet us. I glance around at the groups of assembled spectators. The people want a show. I square my shoulders. I'll do the best I can to give them one.

TWENTY-FIVE

GRACE

As we approach the Colosseum, I'm in awe of its magnificence. I knew it was large from pictures I'd seen in school, but it's much grander than I'd expected. Three stories of arched columns grace the outside. Banners and awnings in bright colors can be seen through the top arches. I can't believe I'm actually here.

Magnus climbs out of the cart, and we follow. Samuel, the driver, pulls the cart away to wait in a different area as more spectators approach the entrance. We stay close together, Scarlet and Matthew and Clara right behind us.

We enter through a stone archway and climb several flights of stone steps. When we walk into the arena, I have to stop for a second in awe. I wish I had my phone and could get a few photos. This place is incredible. Dante takes my arm and we move forward as several people enter behind us. We descend the stairs, heading closer to the arena floor. About ten rows below us are several larger stone seats.

"The Emperor sits there," Magnus whispers. He points to a row to the left. "These are our seats." We file in and sit down. I glance around in awe, and fear at what I'm about to see.

There is a commotion below. The crowd surges to their feet as a man dressed in a green and gold tunic, covered with a gold toga, enters. This must be Emperor Commodus. He's followed by a pretty woman dressed in white. Castillo walks beside her, garbed in a red tunic and toga. My stomach clenches at the sight of him.

They take their seats and servants rush forward with wine and platters of food. I adjust the scarf on my head to conceal part of my face. I'm glad we're several rows above them and mixed in with the crowd. It would be disastrous if Castillo saw us.

A door suddenly opens. I gasp as Christian stumbles into the arena, followed by the pretty Vagary girl I'd seen with him in New Jersey. Clara clasps my hand tightly in hers.

They are dressed in simple tunics and are unarmed. Indignation burns in my chest. How is this a fair fight? I want to rush down there and stop this whole thing, but there is nothing I can do.

The Emperor stands. "Good citizens of Rome. I welcome

you… and ask you if our mighty Gladiator should fight the challengers before us this day?"

"Yes! Silvanus, Silvanus!" The crowd cheers. A small man, a midget really, jumps down from a platform and opens another door. An enormous man, the Gladiator, emerges. I can just imagine what Christian and the Vagary girl must be feeling right now and it makes me sick to my stomach.

The Gladiator, Silvanus, advances on Christian, swinging his sword. Christian dances away. They circle around each other. With the Gladiator's bulk and superior strength, Christian is clearly outmatched. I cringe. How can I possibly rescue him if he's murdered before my eyes? My heart sinks to my toes. This is awful.

Silvanus is a giant of a man. He's all muscles, over six feet tall and bare chested, dressed in a loin cloth and a leather belt. He wears a plumed helmet with a visor and small eye holes along with leather arm and leg armor. He moves toward Christian, unsheathing a wicked looking sword from his belt. A sick feeling moves from my throat and settles in my stomach. I glance at Clara, horrified. She's slowly shaking her head and looks white as a sheet.

A soldier hands a sword to Christian and a dagger to the girl. These weapons seem almost useless against the fierce Gladiator.

Are they both supposed to fighting Silvanus… at the same time? That might be their only advantage. I wish Christian had a shotgun, or maybe a hand grenade or two. Maybe if we had brought Elena and her C4, we might stand a chance.

Silvanus glances at the Vagary girl, quickly dismissing her as a threat, and focuses on Christian. Christian spreads his legs, grasping the sword with both hands in front of him. Silvanus steps toward him and swings his sword. Christian skips out of the way as the sword swishes by, inches from his head. Christian spins around, but Silvanus is fast and their swords meet. He's strong too, his muscles bulging as he pushes Christian backwards. Christian dances away, his boxing expertise kicking in. They parry back and forth, swords clanging. The crowd grows restless around me. Ugh. They want blood.

Silvanus swings his sword again, pushing Christian backwards. Silvanus swings again, and again, with a barbaric yell, as Christian meets his sword time after time, before jumping out of the way. Christian kicks his leg in a round house move, landing a blow to Silvanus's back. The Gladiator grunts, but barely moves. Christian spins around just as Silvanus's sword clangs against his own. I shudder at the grind of metal on metal. Christian is tiring. I can see it in the desperation on his face. It won't be long before he loses this fight.

"Can't we do something?" I whisper to Dante. He glances my way and shakes his head.

"I'm sorry, my dear," Magnus whispers, "There are too many soldiers here. If you try to intervene you'll only get yourselves killed."

I turn back to the arena in time to see Silvanus swing once more, meeting Christian's sword with a mighty thwack and it flies out of his hand. Christian falls to the ground on his back. The Vagary girl screams. Several times, I'd hoped she might throw her dagger at the Gladiator. I silently plead with her to do something, but the battle is happening quickly and she doesn't have a clear shot.

Silvanus stands over Christian. He raises his sword for the death blow, then suddenly stops, chest heaving. He slowly lowers his arm and steps forward.

Clara squeezes my hand tightly. I cover my mouth, afraid I'll scream and draw attention to us.

Silvanus suddenly pulls off his helmet, black hair falling to his shoulders. He studies Christian for a moment then bends over and says something to him. Silvanus raises a fist to the crowd, then turns and walks out of the arena. I'm stunned. What just happened? I think maybe he just spared Christian's life. The crowd around us yells their displeasure.

Emperor Commodus stands. "Silvanus has granted mercy to his challenger today. The match will be postponed until tomorrow."

I sigh in relief. I don't know why, but they've been given a rematch. We might have time to get him out of here before tomorrow.

I glance at Clara. She's staring down at the arena, tears in her eyes. She slowly turns to face me, disbelief plain on her face.

"What is it?" I ask.

"Silvanus, the Gladiator…" She trails off, shaking her head. "It can't be…and yet, I know it's true. I know that face. I know that man. Grace, Silvanus is Simon Hayes, your father."

TWENTY-SIX

CHRISTIAN

We've been given a reprieve. Chest heaving, I lay on the ground, stunned. Who is Silvanus and why didn't he kill me when he had the chance?

Hannah rushes to my side and helps me to my feet. I brush the dirt from my palms. The soldiers reappear and motion for us to follow them back underground. I'm not thrilled about returning to our prison, but it's better than being dead. Before he left the arena, Silvanus whispered that he'd come find me. I hope he's not too late, though. Castillo had thought to have Silvanus do the job for him. He wanted us to suffer. I wonder if this is all part of his plan somehow. Waiting another day to fight Silvanus will be more torture heaped upon us. Especially for Hannah.

Something warm trickles down my arm. I watch as several red dots hit the ground soaking into the dirt. I'm bleeding. Silvanus's sword must have grazed my arm sometime during the fight. With the adrenaline coursing through my veins, I never felt a thing. I do now, though, and my arm beings to sting.

We follow the soldiers and reach our little prison room once more. *What? No one's going to bandage my wound?* I think, cynically.

Hannah drops onto the bench and covers her face with shaking hands.

"I thought you were dead," she whispers, raising stricken eyes to mine.

"I thought I was too," I admit. I'm suddenly weak as the adrenalin that had kept me going deserts me.

"Come show me your arm." Hannah pats the bench, "We need to stop the bleeding." She retrieves her black t-shirt from the corner of the room. She tears a strip from the bottom of the shirt and wraps it around my forearm.

"I'm sorry I wasn't able to help you. I didn't know what to do. I was afraid I would hit you by mistake," she says softly, biting her lip.

"Hey, it's alright. You did the only thing you could do… which was to stay alive," I say.

"What happens now?" Hannah asks.

"Silvanus knew I was a Kairos. He noticed my wristwatch. I

would swear he knew what it was. He said he'd come find me. He's not just a Gladiator, Hannah."

"Oh my heck, maybe he can get us out of here," she says, hopefully.

"I don't know, but I'm anxious to talk to him."

The door rattles as the bar is lifted and it opens. Emperor Commodus enters along with Castillo. The soldiers stand outside, but guard the door.

"A very entertaining morning, I must say," Commodus drawls, glancing from me to Hannah.

"Do you fight with as much skill as your friend?" the Emperor asks Hannah, taking in her pale, dirt stained cheeks, and messy hair. He frowns when she just stares at him.

"She doesn't understand Latin," I say quickly.

"Hmm. Well, we will find out tomorrow. There will be *two* of our finest Gladiators in the arena. We don't want a repeat of today's disappointment. Besides, it will be a larger crowd and we must entertain the people."

"Oh. There *will* be a show tomorrow," Castillo says with an evil smile. I swear his eyes practically gleam with malice. "I personally guarantee it."

"Watch them carefully tonight," Castillo tells the soldiers. "Report to me if anyone tries to come near them." He places a coin in each of the guard's hands and they nod quickly. The door is shut and bolted once more. Hannah collapses on the bench.

"That Emperor guy gives me the creeps," she says with a shudder. I nod, totally agreeing with her. Commodus is more of the puppet in this melodrama, I think. For me, Castillo is the real villain. I hope that doesn't make me the hero, because it's a role I'm not comfortable with. I'm just trying to stay alive from one minute to the next.

TWENTY-SEVEN

GRACE

We exit the arena, blending in with the crowd. Clara's hand trembles in mine. I shake my head. I still can't believe it. Simon Hayes, my father, is *alive*. I quickly connect the dots and the common thread in all of this is Castillo. He must have kidnapped Simon years ago and hid him here, in ancient Rome. Over time, Simon became Silvanus, the Gladiator. This rescue mission is becoming more complicated by the minute.

We step onto the cobblestone street and wait for the cart to return. Roman citizens brush past us, unaware of the visitors from the future who walk among them.

"Are you okay?" Dante whispers. He stands close to my side, his hand not far from the dagger hidden beneath his toga.

"Yes. I'm just in shock," I reply. "I didn't expect to find Simon Hayes today." I feel a little guilty, too. Maybe I should have looked for Simon when I searched for Clara. But since he was a Vagary, I assumed he was a bad person. Maybe he was a victim just like Christian.

When the cart arrives, we climb into the back and head toward Magnus's house. We need to regroup and plan our next move. I know what I want to do. I want to gather all the Kindred from Kairos house and bring them here to assist us in freeing Christian… and of course, Simon. We certainly have more evidence now as to who is behind all the terrible things perpetrated by the Vagaries. They say one bad apple can spoil the whole barrel, and I think Xavier Castillo is rotten to the core.

We've almost reached the house when I hear the sound of hooves in the distance. I glance over my shoulder and see two chariots, pulled by large black horses, approaching fast. Crap. We have to get out of here now.

Everyone jumps from the cart and we sprint towards the portal. Miriam rushes from the house, thrusting Excalibur at Dante as he passes.

"Hurry, they're coming," she calls.

"Go inside and bar the door," Magnus instructs Miriam. She hesitates for a second, then rushes into the house.

We run through the orchard and enter the animal pens just as the chariots stop in front of the house. The soldiers jump down and march toward Magnus. He draws his sword. He is vastly outnumbered. There is shouting and the clang of metal as Magnus tries to stop them from reaching us.

I grasp the Ambitus and focus on Kairos house. The portal activates. As the spinning increases, I glance toward the house just as a soldier knocks Magnus' sword from his hand. He staggers back and the soldier thrusts his sword through him, the blade sticking out of his back. Magnus falls forward onto the ground. Mirum rushes from the house. Her scream echo's through the portal as we hurl through time.

When we arrive at Kairos house, Dante holds me close against him. I'm out of breath and sick to my stomach. Magnus died because of us. And what about Miriam? What will happen to her? Did the soldiers murder her like they did Magnus or will she end up in the arena with Christian?

Matthew wipes the sweat from his forehead, dropping the toga to the ground. Scarlet's headscarf was lost somewhere in the rush to escape, and hair hangs in an auburn tangle down her back.

"We have to go back with more Kairos and free Simon and Christian," Clara says. "I'll talk to Vivica." She flings open the door and rushes up the stairs toward Vivica's apartments.

"Are you alright?" Scarlet says, taking in my pale face.

I nod, weakly. I'm not sure what I am. I know that our

mission just became immensely more complicated, though.

"I've got to have a shower. I'll be quick and then we'll plan our next move," Scarlet says.

"I'll get Liam. He'll want to be included in the fight," Matthew says. He heads down to the gym, where Liam can usually be found training.

We enter the grand foyer just as Mom and Henry leave the kitchen. Henry is munching on one of Juanita's churros. They stop and stare at us. I'm sure we look strange, as we're hot and disheveled… and dressed in Roman togas. Dante holds Excalibur in one hand and the Ambitus is clutched in my fist.

"You look funny," Henry giggles, licking sugar from his fingers.

"You've been doing something dangerous, haven't you," Mom says, her tone accusing.

"I've been doing what I have to," I say, defensively. If she knew how dangerous, she'd lock me in my room for a week. I'm not done, either. I'm going back, but this time I'm taking an army with me.

Mom shakes her head and pulls me close. "Promise me you'll be careful," she whispers.

I nod, hugging her back.

Jacob appears at the top of the stairs.

"Dude, how could you go without me?" he says to Dante, bounding down the stairs, two at a time. "Scarlet tells me you need back up. You know I'm in."

We move to the great room. I pull off the length of toga. The events of the last twenty four hours catch up to me and I collapse on the sofa, exhausted. Dante sits down beside me and I curl into his side.

"This is turning into a bigger deal than we thought," Jacob says, rubbing his hands together.

"I'm thoroughly sick of Xavier Castillo, I can tell you that much," Dante says, frowning.

"If we can stop Castillo, maybe Magnus will get his wish after all," I say.

"Magnus?" Jacob asks.

"He is a Kairos from Rome who helped us. Unfortunately, the Vagaries have control of ancient Rome at that time and he desperately wanted to change that," Dante says

"He died fighting the Vagaries who were after us. We escaped because of him."

Alejandro and Elena rush into the room.

"Grace, you're back. What happened? Did you find Christian?" Alejandro says.

"Yes, we found him, but it's going to take an army to get him out of there," Dante says, and explains where Christian is being held and everything that happened.

"He has a Vagary girl with him. She made an enemy of Castillo. I like her already," I joke.

"Yeah, that guy is loco," Alejandro says, shaking his head and making a circle by his head, the universal sign for crazy.

"I wouldn't want to be a Vagary right about now," Elena says. "It seems like Castillo has got a screw loose." She perches on the end of the sofa.

"Sometimes, the responsibility of leadership can make one take unnecessary risks," Vivica says from the doorway. We all turn at the sound of her voice. Clara stands beside her.

"Clara told me what happened today and I must say I am surprised at the depravity of Castillo, especially as it involves Simon, his nephew," Vivica says.

"Castillo was always jealous of Simon," Clara says. "Simon was quite popular, especially with the younger generation of Vagaries. He had some radical ideas for changing the way they ran their organization. When Castillo found out about our relationship, he decided to take action against Simon. So Simon told me to meet him in Paris and we would make plans to escape. Unfortunately, he never showed up. I never saw him again… until today."

"I contacted Nikolai, the head of Russia's Kairos. He has graciously agreed to lend us his elite fighting team to assist us with this matter. They are twelve of the Kairo's best warriors, trained for special circumstances such as this," Vivica says, glancing at her watch. "They will be here within the hour. I have been patient and used restraint with the Vagaries and Xavier Castillo for decades. The time for patience is over. The time for action has arrived."

I squeeze Dante's hand tightly, relieved that Vivica is with us.

"Ricardo and James are seeking volunteers from the rest of the Kairos in the United States. They're expecting another twenty five Kindred to join us."

Vivica glances around at our group. Relief floods through me. I think we're all in shock that we finally have the support from Vivica and the Kairos community that we need.

"What are you waiting for?" Vivica says, raising one perfectly sculpted eyebrow. "Go prepare. We leave in one hour."

We scramble to our feet and dash from the room.

Mom and Henry enter the room as the others rush out. She pulls me down on the sofa. Henry climbs onto my lap, like he used to when he was little. My arms tighten around him.

"I don't really understand what's going on, Grace, but I want you to know that we love you," Mom says. I nod, my eyes filling with tears.

"Please be safe, alright…" she adds, wiping a tear form her eyes. I nod and hold Henry tightly. He allows this for a few seconds before wiggling free.

"Come on," Mom says, standing and holding out her hand to Henry. "let's go to the back garden for lessons today."

Henry nods, and waves to me as they exit through the French doors onto the back patio. Dante pulls me to my feet and looks me over.

"I want to get you more protective clothing for this mission," he says.

I nod in agreement. Since I could be facing Roman soldiers,

perhaps I need my own armor. I take the stairs down to the gym, Dante behind me. I have the Ambitus, and all the ancient artifacts, but I decide a Kevlar vest is in order…better to be safe than sorry.

I'm zipping up the vest when Dante says, "You don't have to go today, Grace. You've already done enough. You've located Christian and found Simon. Let us take care of this. I don't want you anywhere near this battle."

I gaze into Dante's eyes, so full of concern, and sigh. I know he doesn't want to see me hurt.

"I realize you want to protect me, and I thank you for that," I say, reaching up and softly kiss his lips. He pulls me into his embrace, hugging me tightly. I relax in his arms for a moment and savor his warmth.

"This is something I have to do," I say, softly. "Because I'm the only one who has the ability to activate the Ambitus, and use the power of the artifacts, I have to be there. I don't want to lose you either, Dante, but if I can make a difference to our success, I have to go."

He nods reluctantly, but the concern in his eyes tells me he doesn't like my answer.

On my way up to my room, the front door opens and Jacob and Jillian enter the foyer. She rushes over and hugs me tight.

"So, where's the party?" Jillian asks, her arms folded across her chest. I stammer and look around.

"Party?" I ask, confused?

"Something big is about to go down, isn't it?" she whispers, eyes bright. "I mean, the courtyard is full of guys that look like WWE wrestlers."

I glance out of the window, and sure enough there are a dozen guys as big as houses, standing by the fountain. I suppress a giggle when I notice Avery in the middle of the group, flirting with several at one time.

"That must be Russia's Elite fighting team. Why are they waiting outside? Shouldn't you invite them in?" I ask Jacob.

"Juanita tried, but they took one look at the house and said they'd wait in the courtyard." He shrugs. "I think they're afraid they might break something."

The foyer begins to fill with Kairos. Liam, Scarlet and Matthew enter followed by Clara, Vivica and Quinton. Ricardo and James, Alejandro, Trina and Elena enter with ten more Kairos I've never seen before. I'm not sure how we will all fit in the portal.

"We'll travel in two groups," Vivica says, answering my question.

"Grace, you will take each group through the portal to the destination. Upon arrival, you will secure them in a safe location and return for the other group. Once we are all together, we will proceed to the arena."

"What about clothing for the time period?" I ask.

"I've got that covered," she says, "Tunics and togas large enough to wear over our own clothing are waiting in the library."

As everyone crowds into the library, I retrieve my costume from the great room where I left it in a heap in the corner. I drape it over my clothing. It's slightly wrinkled and uncomfortable, with the added layer of the Kevlar vest. I have too many thoughts spinning around my mind to worry about it, though.

Jillian pulls me aside. "Listen to me, Grace Bennet, you better the hell come back, you hear me?" She squeezes me tight, then turns and walks over to stand beside Jacob. I smile. I love that girl.

It takes another fifteen minutes before we're finally ready. I glance around the foyer. We look like a bunch of college students going to a frat party. I shake my head. I hope we can pull this off without freaking out some innocent Roman citizens.

Vivica and Quinton, Clara, Alejandro and Elena are in the first group along with several Kairos I haven't met formally. Dante and I stand in the middle of the room. Everyone grasps the arm of the person next to them, forming a chain. Luckily, I don't have to use all the artifacts like the first time as I know where Christian is located. I'm relieved I can leave them in Vivica's safe. I focus on Rome and that particular point in history.

As soon as the first group is situated in a secure location, I'll return for the second group. I glance out of the open door and notice a couple in the corner of the foyer, locked in a tight embrace. They step apart, and I smile as I realize it's Jacob and

Jillian. Cheeks slightly pink, Jacob enters the portal, closing the door firmly behind him. I clutch the Ambitus to my chest. It's time to bring Christian and Simon home.

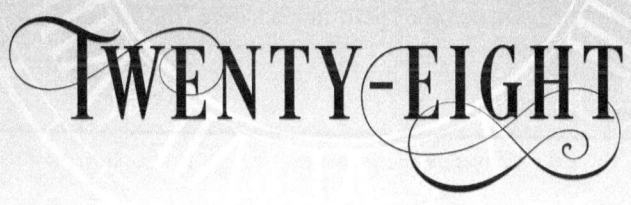

TWENTY-EIGHT

CHRISTIAN

I jolt awake and sit up quickly. There it is again, a low scraping noise just outside the wooden door. Someone is out there. Hannah stirs, and opens her eyes.

"What is it?" she whispers.

"Shhh," I place my finger over my lips.

I hear a soft grunt and a rustling sound. Someone is at the door. I wish I had a knife, or a weapon of some kind. We're sitting ducks in here.

A moment later the door swings open and the large frame of Silvanus fills the doorway, back lit by several torches in the corridor.

"I can't stay long," he says. "I bribed the guard to look the other way, but the patrol guards will be by here in a few moments."

Silvanus enters and Hannah scoots across the floor to the wall. I forgot she doesn't understand what he just said.

"It's okay. He's not going to hurt us," I say, quickly. She nods, but stays by the wall.

"Ah, English," Silvanus smiles broadly, "It's been an age since I've heard anyone speak my language," he replies in English, but with a strong Latin accent. Hannah gasps, and slowly stands.

"I'm called Silvanus the gladiator, here in Rome, but my real name is Simon Hayes. I'm from Manhattan, New York. I've been stuck here for the last eighteen years. I can't tell you how happy I am to see you."

I shake my head. I can't believe it. Silvanus, the great gladiator, is from New York City. Incredible.

"I know who you are. Every Vagary is taught about you," Hannah says, her tone disbelieving. "I was told you betrayed the Vagaries and were lost in a time stop trying to escape to the future."

"You are a Vagary, also?" Simon asks.

"Yes, I am.. well, I was." Hannah shrugs. "Christian is a Kairos."

Simon studies us both for a moment, then turns to me. "Why did Castillo bring you here to die in the arena?"

"It's complicated," I say, shrugging. "Basically, Castillo hoped to trade me for another Kairos. When that didn't happen, I was brought here. Hannah, doesn't deserve any of this. Castillo decided he didn't like her attitude towards me and brought her along."

Simon shakes his head. "My uncle has always been power hungry and a bit crazy, if you ask me. Your story sounds all too familiar. When Castillo found out I'd taken money from the Vagaries and hidden it, he was furious. He couldn't kill me though, or he'd never find the money. He brought me here thinking I'd give in and confess, but instead I flourished. I soon became a favorite with the Emperor and the Roman people. By then it was too late, so he left me here to rot. Every so often, he shows up hoping I'll have had enough and tell him what he wants." Simon shrugs, rubbing his hand down his face.

"If it was only *me* involved, I'd have said to hell with it and given him the money. But there are others that could be hurt by him, so I've kept my mouth shut. I've tried for years to find a portal, but this is a large country, and unless I stumbled upon it somehow, I'd never find one."

"But there is a portal in the Colosseum," Hannah says. "Castillo used it to bring us here."

Simon moves closer. "Where is it? Could you take me to it?" he asks, his eyes searching Hannah's intently. She shakes her head.

I glance at Hannah. "I'm not sure where it is, either. I'd have to walk around the arena and look at the different rooms to see if anything is familiar. Lino knows where it is, though.

He was there when we arrived with Castillo and took us to the Emperor."

"Lino, the little snake, would sell his own mother if it meant a coin in his pocket," Simon says, shaking his head. He glances over his shoulder. "Maybe I can persuade him." He rubs his neck and sighs, suddenly looking tired.

"I just wanted you to know that the Emperor plans to give the people a good show tomorrow so he's ordered another Gladiator in the arena with me. Claudius is a blood thirsty and a ruthless competitor. He hates to lose. A squadron of soldiers will be in attendance also. I'm not sure if it's possible, but I'll try to keep you alive. I hope they train the Vagaries and Kairos to fight like they did in my day. If they do, you might have a chance." He glances behind him. "I have to go now. I'll see you tomorrow and pray that we are victorious."

He turns and leaves the room, latching the bar behind him. I had hoped he would take us with him right now and we could search for the portal and get the hell out of here, but the place is crawling with soldiers. We probably wouldn't get very far anyway.

Simon Hayes. I shake my head. I swear I've heard that name before, but I can't think where. I lay down on the hard ground again and Hannah sits beside me. My back protests and I roll on my side.

"We're going to die tomorrow, aren't we?" Hannah says softly.

"Not if I can help it," I reply, with more conviction than I actually feel. "Try to get some sleep, okay."

"I'll try. I know you're trying to make this easier for me, Christian. Thank you," Hannah says. She sighs, and moves around next to me in an effort to find a semi-comfortable spot.

I doubt I'll sleep. Instead, I send a silent SOS to the Kairos in New York City and hope they receive it.

TWENTY-NINE

GRACE

The first group of Kairos arrives safely in Rome and I hide them in Magnus' barn. It's early morning and the sun just crests the mountains to the east. Good. We have time to organize before the fight in the Colosseum at midday. I scan the area, but see no sign of Miriam, or their servant, Samuel. Heart pounding, I walk back to the portal alone. As far as I can tell, no one is watching, except for my Kindred in the barn as I travel back to Kairos house once more. I try not to think about what could be happening to Christian and Simon. There is no time to lose as the second group is waiting.

Raymond, Trina, Avery, Scarlet, Matthew, James and Ricardo stand in the foyer, along with the elite fighting team. There will be twenty of us in the portal. A tight fit in the small room, but we'll make it work. Once they are all in place, I activate the portal with the Ambitus. We spin through time, arms locked together. The sun is high in the sky when we arrive. We must have been gone longer than I had anticipated.

"Thank God, you're back," Dante says, "I was beginning to worry. You've been gone for hours."

"I was only gone a few minutes." I stare at the Ambitus in my hand. Don't fail me now, I think, a little desperately.

The little cart is parked by the barn, but we'll never fit this many people inside it anyway. We'll never make it before the event starts in the Coliseum if we walk. Plus, how will this large group get close to the arena without being stopped?

"I remember Magnus saying there were portals closer to the arena, but they were controlled by the Vagaries," I say to Dante. "Could we travel to one of them? With this large group surely we can handle any Vagaries we find."

"It seems we have no choice," Vivica says, sounding annoyed that I had taken so long to return.

I shrug. It wasn't my fault that the Ambitus decided to choose this moment to act up.

I motion everyone to gather closely around me once more. I'm not sure how large this portal actually is and I don't want anyone to be left behind. I glance at the faces around me. These people, these Kindred, have become my family. I close my eyes and pray we make it safely through the battle that lies in front of us. Please work, I silently beg the Ambitus, and grasp it in both hands. The portal activates and once more we fly through time.

THIRTY

CHRISTIAN

It's time. We're marched along the same route as before, past the animal pens and to the doors leading to the arena. The guards hand us our weapons before we climb the stairs.

It's a warm, but windy day and the banners overhead snap in the breeze as we walk into the arena. The crowd cheers, while some boo and chant, "Silvanus, Silvanus." They want their hero. They don't know anything about us, supposing we're criminals, or captive warriors from a distant battle.

Like yesterday, the Emperor sits on his throne, his wife by his side. Castillo stands as we enter and raises his silver wine goblet in a mocking toast. As if to say, here's to you, and the entertainment we will receive today.

I glance at Hannah. She stands stiffly, chin high, the dagger clutched in a white knuckle grip. I'm actually really proud of her. She's handled herself well, in a terrifying situation. It's not over yet, though.

Lino opens the door, and I expect Simon to enter the arena, but it's a different Gladiator. This must be Claudius. He's as big as Simon, but without the good looks. This guy is scarred, with a crooked nose, from being broken too many times, and a bald head. He doesn't even bother with a helmet. His breast plate and leg armor are all the protection he wears. The way he stares at Hannah and myself, I know he won't hesitate to kill us. This is his sport and he means to win.

Simon enters the arena next, looking as fierce as ever. I don't know how he will protect us from Claudius, unless he plans to fight the other Gladiator himself. When he pulls his sword from his belt and faces Claudius, I realize that's exactly what he's going to do.

The crowd goes wild. They cheer, each one calling for their favorite Gladiator to prevail. Claudius smiles, as if he's been wanting the chance to fight the great Silvanus.

I motion for Hannah to step back against the arena wall. I want her out of the way of swinging swords or flying daggers.

With a yell, Simon rushes Claudius. He steps to the side as their swords clank sharply against each other. They fight furiously, their blows meant to kill. I have to give Simon credit, he's a skilled fighter. As they circle and parry, Claudius sees a break and taking it, thrusts his sword at Simon. He misses his torso, but grazes his upper arm and blood wells up, dripping onto the ground. The crowd cheers wildly, excited at the first sight of blood.

Simon doesn't let it get to him, though, and advances on Claudius. Claudius turns and catches a battle-axe thrown to him by Lino, who chortles with glee. He now has two weapons against Simon's one. Not a fair fight. Fury whips through me, hot like a poker. I'm sick of this whole damn thing.

"Stay here," I say to Hannah with a growl and move to stand beside Simon, sword at the ready.

Simon nods as I approach, a slow grin spreading across his face. Claudius looks surprised for a moment and then shrugs as if to say I can take you both. Maybe he can, but I'm going to make it as difficult as possible.

We charge and Claudius wields the battle-axe from one side to the other, effectively pushing us backwards. I circle around him, hoping to get him from behind. A door opens to my right and another Gladiator enters the arena. He's a tall, muscular man, with a ruddy complexion and mean eyes. He's covered with a breastplate and armor on his legs and arms. His sword is twice the size of mine. I whirl around as he runs my way. He yells, and he swings his sword. The only advantage I have is that I'm fast. I jump out of the way, barely, as his sword brushes past my shoulder. Mean eyes turns, and snarls like a rabid dog. I dance away and he follows, his heavy armor making him slow. He advances and I'm nearly against the wall when a dagger whizzes past my head, sinking deep into mean eyes shoulder, just outside of his armor. He falls to his knees, shrieking in pain.

I glance over at Hannah. She shrugs, smiling.

"Good shot," I call.

She has no weapon now, which concerns me. I run to mean eyes and finish him off, thrusting my sword deep in his gut. He falls to the ground. I remove Hannah's dagger from his body. The spectators gasp and boo, but some yell encouragement, cheering for the underdogs in the fight. Simon and Claudius continue to spar, but they're well-matched.

Emperor Commodus raises his fist and the crowd goes quiet. The fighting stops and Simon strides over to stand beside me, sweat dripping down his face.

Commodus motions to the guards standing on either side the doors we came through earlier. They open, and five soldiers enter the arena. I cross to Hannah and hand her back the dagger. The weapon is not much use now. As the soldiers advance, I notice several of them wear the Vagary ruby ring. These are no ordinary Roman soldiers. Castillo is behind this, and it's clear we won't be getting out of here alive.

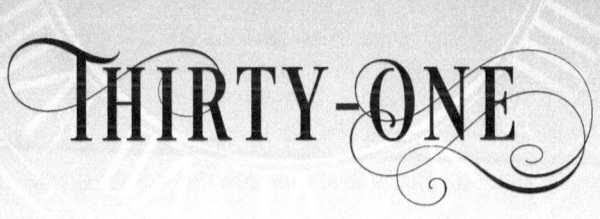

THIRTY-ONE

GRACE

We land in a dark and musty room that smells of animals. It's tight with everyone inside the small space, but we all made it.

The distant sound of cheering brings my focus back to the task before us. Dante and I weave through our Kindred and peer out the opening to a dim corridor.

"This is the Hypogeum, the area under the Colosseum," Dante says.

"The battle has already begun," Clara says. "We have to get out there before it's too late."

We move as quietly as we can, heading toward the sounds of the crowd. They grow louder as we near a set of large wooden doors. It's surreal to be here, under the Colosseum, about to go to battle against the Vagaries. I grip the Ambitus and it flares to life, green energy pulsating through my hand, up my arm and finally surrounding me. I'm filled with a sense of purpose. This moment is why the dagger choose me.

I nod to Dante, and he motions for everyone to be ready.

With a battle cry we rush up the stairs and into the light of the arena. The crowd goes quiet, in shock at this turn of events.

I focus on Christian. He stands in front of us, the Vagary girl and Simon on either side of him. Five Roman solders march toward them, swords ready. One minute delay and we might have been too late. Christian glances over his shoulder. He nods, and a huge grin spreads across his face as we approach.

"What took you so long?" he calls. I'm so relieved we arrived in time, I can hardly speak. I step toward him, and almost trip on the cloth wrapped around me. It's clear I can't fight in this togas, so I rip mine from around me and throw it to the side. My fellow Kairos do the same, leaving a pile of clothing behind us. My stomach is in knots, but a calm settles over me. I can do this. *We* can do this, together, my Kindred family and I. The fact that Dante has taken my hand and is holding it firmly, doesn't hurt.

The crowd murmurs and points. I don't care. Let them think whatever they want. I'm here to rescue my Kindred and that's exactly what I'm going to do. More Roman Soldiers pour out of the corridors into the arena. This fight wouldn't be as easy as I had hoped.

I glance to the right and notice Castillo, dressed in his Roman robes, sitting next to the Emperor. His eyes bulge and he looks around wildly. Oh no you don't, I think. Two guards close rank around the Emperor, effectively blocking Castillo's exit. I nod in satisfaction. You're not getting away that easy.

With a roar, the soldiers in front of us raise their swords and run toward our group. We join Christian and Simon. Yells erupt as we charge into battle. Around me the fighting rages in a cacophony of screams and clashing of metal, but my focus remains steadily on the soldier in front of me. He raises his sword, about to cut me down, but I focus the green energy of the Ambitus, and it flies from my hand, finding its mark, deep in his neck. The soldier falls to the ground. I retrieve the dagger and Dante is behind me in an instant. He hands me a dropped sword, and I grimace at the blood dripping off the blade. Dante positions himself so that we fight back to back. The ear splitting clang of clashing metal is almost deafening. My arm strains as I swing the heavy weapon, but the adrenaline coursing through my body gives me the strength I need.

A soldier lunges toward me, and once again the Ambitus finds his throat. The dagger won't allow my opponents to get too close, and I'm grateful for the protection.

The Russian's move into teams, fighting a single soldier in pairs, slaying them and moving on to the next. The Emperor is on his feet, seemingly delighted at this unexpected show.

Castillo begins inching backwards, looking for a way out.

"Over there," I yell to Dante, pointing to Castillo. We begin to edge closer to where he stands. I want a clear shot at him.

The Vagary girl fights fiercely with a sword and dagger. She dances around a soldier, her martial arts skill make her fast on her feet. Alejandro and Elena make short work of the their opponents and move on to the next. Trina and Avery work together. They look like Ninja goddesses come to life, distracting the soldiers with their tight leather pants and gorgeous figures as well as their martial arts skills, they end the confused soldiers with their daggers.

Liam and Matthew have joined Simon. They surround a Roman Gladiator, his huge size equal to Liam's. The Gladiator drops his sword, and tries to flee the arena. The crowd boos, unhappy at his retreat.

"Claudius, Claudius, they chant." A Roman soldier steps in front of the Gladiator, Claudius, swinging a battle axe, effectively removing his head from his body. The crowd goes wild. I swallow down the bile that threatens and focus on the task at hand. I duck as a battle axe swings by my head.

As we move within range of Castillo, the Emperor raises his fist and the soldiers retreat, standing down, and moving away from the Kairos. They have lost half their numbers, and dead soldiers lay scattered across the arena floor.

The Emperor stares at Dante and I for a moment before saying, "Travelers, I believe you have come here to claim one of your own." He points to Christian.

I nod, my chest heaving as I catch my breath and look around.

Hannah stands on one side of the arena, next to Simon. Christian is on the other side, having been separated by the battle.

My heart drops as I notice Quinton kneeling on the arena floor. He holds Vivica in his arms, her body limp as blood pools beneath her. Clara kneels beside him. I long to rush to their sides, but now is not the time. I face Emperor Commodus, once more.

"You have fought bravely." He twists the ruby ring on his index finger. I was told the Emperor wasn't a Vagary and I hope that information is correct.

"Perhaps they have come for you also, Castillo, as you brought the Kairos prisoners to our city," the Emperor says.

"I'll leave you to deal with the Kairos as you see fit. I'll take my leave now," Castillo says, bowing and edging past the guards toward the arena exit.

"Why hurry off so quickly? The fun is just beginning," Commodus says, gesturing to the guards, who grab Castillo and hold him in place.

The Emperor rubs his hands together, obviously delighted at the turn of events.

He motions to the guards and they march Castillo down the steps and onto the arena floor. Castillo stands before Dante and I, with the rest of our Kindred behind us. He has no weapon and looks terrified, as suddenly the tables have turned.

"Grace, I had hoped we could extend our family association," Castillo says, nervously, hand outstretched.

"Like you did with Simon, or should I say Silvanus?" I ask.

Castillo's face goes white and he stammers. Suddenly, he lunges, and grabs a sword where it lay a few feet from him. He waves it in front of him, familiar with the weapon, as he's been a Vagary his whole life.

Dante steps forward, sword raised, ready to do battle, but I move in front of him, the Ambitus clutched tightly in my hand.

"You are *not* my family," I say, clearly, my voice raised above the murmur of the crowd.

The green energy throbs and expands around me. The Ambitus shakes in my hand, eager to find it's mark in my enemy.

Castillo glances from my face to my hand. His eyes widen as he takes in the Ambitus. Fear and greed war across his face. *You want this? I think.* I glance from the dagger to him. *You can have it then.* I open my palm and the dagger flies from my hand, landing in the middle of Castillo's forehead. He stumbles back, surprise briefly crossing his features before he crumples to the ground.

The arena erupts in shouts and cheers. Commodus motions to the soldiers guarding him and they exit the Colosseum.

The citizens are ushered from the arena also, as the remaining soldiers retreat, leaving only my Kindred on the arena floor.

I rush to Vivica, but it's too late. She is gone, her body limp in Quinton's arms. The leader of New York's Kairos is dead. Tears sting my eyes. Vivica and I may not have always seen eye to eye, but I respected her knowledge and leadership. She was my Kindred.

"I couldn't reach her in time," Quinton says, his voice thick with emotion.

I stroke his back, my heart breaking for my friend.

"How long were you together?" I ask.

"We were married… sixty-three years ago in Vienna," he stammers, and buries his face in her hair.

I slowly stand as the other Kindred gather around Vivica to pay their respect.

I notice Christian walking purposefully across the arena towards the Vagary girl. She stands awkwardly in the middle of the Kairos Kindred. She holds a dagger in her hand, blood dripping down her face from a cut on her forehead. Christian drops his sword as he reaches her and stares into her eyes. He gently wipes the blood from her cheek. She smiles up at him right before his mouth finds hers in a long, passionate kiss. She flings her arms around his neck and they melt into each other.

Well, I wasn't expecting that, I think, but I smile. I'm happy for my friend. I glance around and see Simon standing next to Clara. They are talking earnestly, heads close together. Tears fill my eye, as I see my parents together for the first time. Dante squeezes my hand and I smile up at him through my tears.

Dante turns to everyone and calls, "We must return immediately to Kairos house. We will mourn our leader there."

We band together once more to head back to the portal. My emotions are all over the place as they course through me. We were victorious, in more ways than I expected. We rescued Christian and defeated Castillo, once and for all. I'm not foolish enough to think that our conflicts with the Vagaries are over, but I'm relieved for now. With Vivica's death, the Kairos will need to reorganize and elect a new leader. I fully expect it will be Dante. I lean into him, his arm closing around me as the Kairos crowd into the portal, arms linked once more and we travel home.

THIRTY-TWO

CHRISTIAN

Hannah places another slice of chocolate cake on my plate. I shake my head, but take a bite anyway. As soon as we arrived back at Kairos house, Juanita had a huge meal ready and waiting.

She was devastated when she saw Vivica and collapsed in Quinton's arms. She cried for several minutes, before her motherly instincts kicked in and she insisted on feeding everyone. It's the way she shows her love for us.

Hannah was welcomed with open arms. She fought alongside the Kairos, and now she's considered one of us. Avery and Trina enter the kitchen.

"When is Vivica's funeral?" Avery asks, plopping down in the seat beside Grace.

"Quinton says next week. She'll be buried on the Kairos's private island," Grace replies.

"Is Dante going the be the new leader in New York?" Trina asks.

"I don't know, it will be decided by secret ballet," Grace says.

"I'll bet it's you, Grace," Trina says, before reaching for a slice of cake.

"Me? No, I'm still a new Kairos. I'm sure Dante will be elected." Grace says, shaking her head.

I wonder, though. Already, the Kairos are asking Grace for advice and want to know all about the ancient artifacts and how the Ambitus works. I shrug, and take another bite of cake, smiling at Hannah.

We leave the kitchen and head out to the back garden. The sun warms my shoulders as Hannah slips her hand in mine. I never thought a month ago, when I was sitting in a prison cell in Kansas City, that I would end up here, holding the hand of this beautiful girl.

We sit on the ground, the spring sunshine warming the grass.

"I need to call my dad and tell him everything that happened. He'll be shocked and probably want me to come home." Hannah raises her chin and shrugs. "I'm going to tell him I'm a Kairos now, and he'll just have to accept it."

"You might be surprised. I hear that Simon retuning from

the dead and the Vagaries finding out Castillo was behind it has shaken up the their organization."

Hannah nods, and we glance up as Dante and Grace approach.

"I thought we'd find you here," Grace says, and sits on the grass beside us. "Dante and I are going on a little trip and I wanted you to know so you wouldn't worry about us."

"You'll hear all about it when we return." Dante says, holding out his hand and helping Grace to her feet. I watch as they walk away, hand in hand, heads close together. Those feelings that I had for Grace have changed to friendship and I'm fine with that. I have deeper ones for Hannah now. Whatever happens next, I finally feel like it will be okay.

"Want to work out in the gym?" I ask as we get to our feet.

"Race you there," she says, and darts away. I make a grab for her and she shrieks, her laughter echoing behind her as we race to the house.

EPILOGUE

I step onto the cobblestone sidewalk, Lake Lucerne shimmering in the distance. I stare at the receipt in my hand and shake my head. I still can't believe it's real. Simon Hayes really hid millions of dollars in my name in a bank in Switzerland. Over the years the amount swelled to nearly 100 million dollars. It's now been wired to a bank in New York and I'll decide what to do with it from there. I know several charities that would benefit from some of the money.

"Are you alright?" Dante asks, his gorgeous blue eyes studying my face.

I nod, at a loss for words at the moment, which has got to be a first for me. Dante slips his hand in mine, and we cross the street to gaze at the water. The spring wind picks up and blows my hair across my face. Dante tucks a strand behind my ear and slips his arm around me. I sigh, glad that my Kindred are back safely in New York. Things are quiet…for now, anyway.

Simon and Clara are working on renewing their relationship. They've been through a lot, having been separated for years, but they seem determined to put the past behind them.

I'm not sure what will happen next with the Kairos, but I know Dante and I have time to figure things out… all the time in the world.

THE END

ACKNOWLEDGEMENTS

I have so many people to thank for this book. My readers, who inspire me to keep writing every day. Also, my husband, Ross Hopkin, for being patient with me while I bury my face in my laptop for hours. I'd also like to thank my daughter Nina Walker for encouraging me to follow my dreams and never give up. My talented cover designer, Lori Grundy, and my editor Jeni Chappell get another big thank you.

ABOUT THE AUTHOR

K.S. HALL splits her time between the mountains of northern Utah and the red rocks of southern Utah. She is mother to twelve and grandmother to many more. She's also an avid traveler, reader, puzzle master, and of course, writer.

WWW.KARRENHALL.COM

www.ingramcontent.com/pod-product-compliance
Lightning Source LLC
Chambersburg PA
CBHW030324180626
46810CB00003B/1220